Born and bred in the countryside, now living in the west Yorkshire Dales. Anthony Phillips enjoys DIY, gardening, church bell ringing, choral, harmony singing and barbershop singing. He spent most of his working life in agriculture, horticulture and arboriculture, both as a worker and more recently, as a lecturer in organic horticulture, rural studies and playing field/golf course management.

To A. Joan

Anthony Phillips

---

# HALF MOON HOUSE

AUSTIN MACAULEY PUBLISHERS™

LONDON • CAMBRIDGE • NEW YORK • SHARJAH

A CIP catalogue record for this title is available from the British Library.

ISBN 9781035840724 (Paperback)
ISBN 9781035840731 (ePub e-book)

www.austinmacauley.co.uk

First Published 2024
Austin Macauley Publishers Ltd®
1 Canada Square
Canary Wharf
London
E14 5AA

Throughout the brilliant starlight night watch, security guards could see twinkling stars and streamers from shooting the day broke the eggshell of a golden sun the ghost of the moon with its sharp tips still hung in the West. The green expanse of lawn would soon see the nation's greatest auction in just a few hours' time with marquees and men of burden carrying, wheeling in and out the various designated tents to be placed on show and then later go under the variety of auctioneer's hammers.

Hordes of onlookers, nosey parkers, interested buyers and conveyancing solicitors ready to act on behalf of whomsoever would pay their high fees, were beginning to stream through the open gates.

Just as in better days Royalty and people of the upper echelons of society had enjoyed the expansive view as they sped through the massive gates and up the gravel drive in horse drawn coaches and of late, in chauffeur-driven limousines. It was now the turn of the world and his wife to enjoy the grandiose views of the castle-like house and pristine gardens. People were turning up from everywhere, some to bid, others there to watch the fun as auction fever sets in and make a fool of themselves, or of course bag the bargain of the day. Some even dressed up just to be part of the spectacle and possibly get their names in the national papers or be pictured in the national news. This was the biggest single sale of a property being broken up by the state because no one wanted the white elephant of repairing and maintaining such a large estate, not even the state itself.

Five marquees were being quickly erected, each with a rostrum and chairs facing it. A team of auctioneers would be on call to give a continuity of lots. At the entrance to each marquee, was a portable banking unit with one or other of the high street banks in attendance to aid and assist with the transfer of monies.

There were cables from a Tanoy system all over the lawns and patios, some pinned down and some just gaffer taped to whatever.

Sophisticated satellite connections and vans parked willy nilly everywhere, and people had been pouring into the site for the last three hours. Screens were in place with pictures from the other auction rooms.

A high-profile security system of people and communications was set up alongside the public address system with interconnecting phone lines for some registered customers to bid remotely.

Complemented by three mobile restaurants of sorts with their plastic tables, cups, cutlery and rubbish bins; the latter seemed to be a receptacle for target practice, not showing much promise of careful aims.

The gardens were heaving with people, the gardeners with visible tears in their eyes at the mayhem they might have to repair. The nearby fields were a temporary car park and all security

Staff had strict instructions that no vehicle of any kind was to pass through the gates until the auction was completed, allowing for careful scrutinisation of lots at the end of each daily session and early morning for some.

The Tanoy system burst into life crackling and whistling but when calm, they heralded the start.

"My Lords, Ladies and Gentleman, Drewson and Chambers Auction house of Littlejohn Street, Brewald North Wales extend a warm welcome to all here today and thank you for attending. The sale will commence in Marquee ONE with the Auction of the fine house and accompanying buildings as in the catalogues in all salerooms. These catalogues are on sale at two pounds each and, no doubt for some of you, will form part of a collection in years to come. Each entrance and exit have a steward who will be in an orange tabard. He or she is there to direct you

It is expected that the sale will last for three days and please note the conditions of sale are posted in all appropriate places. Please also be aware that any non-completed sales due to lack of funds will carry a penalty of four percent of the hammer price per month until completion. No goods can be taken from the saleroom until the days auction is complete which will be as near as 3 o'clock as possible. Alternatively, goods may be taken after 8 o'clock until 10 o'clock each morning. Please ensure that no vehicles are left in the grounds between those times. There are adequate parking places as directed. All goods must be removed by two days after completion of the sale unless specifically organised with us the auctioneers.

Thank you all for your attention, the sale will commence in ten minutes. Your auctioneers for the day will be myself, Geoffrey Poole, and my colleagues are Roger Greenaway, Paul Camsel, Heather Hutchinson, Avril Strackfield, Steve

Asquatti, Michael Wildeman and John Wardhay. When not actually on the rostrum they will be in one of our three offices here to assist you."

The musical interlude led to a buzz of people all talking and went on until the auctioneer began again.

"Now, we begin ladies and gentlemen, with the main great house and accompanying buildings included in the courtyard as per the catalogue and the surrounding seventeen acres totalling twenty-two acres in all. All is designated in the legal packages and the catalogues which are available in the entrances to each saleroom and the office.

Now where shall we start...say four million pounds? Thank you, sir."

A gasp went round the room.

"I have four million, four million five hundred thousand, thank you, madam, five million, thank you, sir, and five hundred, thank you, madam. Six million! Thank you, sir. Madam? No? Then I have six million thank you. Any further bids? Then if no further bids going once, going twice, and for the...six million and five hundred thousand on the telephone...Are you coming back sir? No, then I have six million five hundred thousand once, twice, and for the final time, gone to the telephone bidder." Geoffrey was amazed how speedily the commission was earned on one item in three minutes flat.

Paddle No. 345 came up time after time buying all the properties in close proximity to the main house, no one seemed to know where and from whom the bidding was coming from but money was of no consequence. Already some of the local 'landed' gentry had left obviously content in the knowledge that their new neighbour was indeed of some moneyed background.

The hall had been put at the disposal of the auctioneer's staff for the three days and a lot of champagne and 'nibbles' were taken advantage of. Even the breakfast was fit for royalty, certainly for a reasonably priced menu at the makeshift all-day cafe.

By nine thirty the following day, car parks were bulging with onlookers and a distinctly a smaller number of chauffeur-driven cars. Today's buyers would be the smallholdings and cottage set, with the final day being mostly cottages and equipment with a few rental properties. For auctioneers, it was good solid commission stuff that often then led to rental incomes as well.

It was the third day that was to change Chris Jenkin's life forever. As local borough surveyor from the age of twenty, over the following twenty years, he had been at the beck and call of this committee and that committee, taking irate calls from council house tenants and generally a dogsbody for any Tom, Dick or Harriet that had a query, usually humdrum about housing in general.

It was no coincidence that seeing the presales literature of one of the nation's biggest estates, he knew there would be an endless stream of telephone questions about what would or wouldn't be possible under present byelaws, with regards to making a dream home out of something they may or may not buy at the auction. It was a bit of a busman's holiday for him and his wife Matty to go trolling around the estate on the last day of the sale, but the whole area was buzzing with rumour. Sitting in one of the outside edge seats, trying to be inconspicuous, someone passed by and brushed his catalogue, the one he managed to get because of his position at work, onto the floor and his attention was drawn to Lot 1117 'Woodland Folly House.' He began reading and was soon engrossed in 'a building of unusual design and character swathed in ivy believed to have begun construction c 1520.' in need of complete modernisation but in a secluded woodland area with access via Melfort Road. There are no mains services and the property has been unoccupied for several years.

"Matty?"

"What now Chris?" she said, bringing her head out of the catalogue.

"Do you fancy a little drive?"

"Not really, we have only just got here."

"I know, dearest, but look at this."

"The old moon houses."

"You know it?"

"Yes, it's haunted… when we were kids, we used to go up there and throw stones into the chimney then run like the clappers, it is only half built by all accounts."

"So?" he persisted.

"What are you thinking now?"

"I am not sure, but as this is a holiday, please bear with me and let's go and have a look at it."

"Will cost you a burger and chips when we get back."

"There it is through those bushes." They scrambled and fought their way up a narrow and steep pathway.

"It is just what I've always wanted," he said quietly to himself.

"What, dear?"

"I think I have fallen in love with this place."

"What, this pile of whatever."

"Yes, can't you see, if we cleared the brambles and stuff there is a driveway, we could have mains services installed and consider what architects do with old barns these days. Think what they could do here." A plea entered into the conversation.

"You ARE SERIOUS!"

"Matty dearest, if it wasn't for the time factor against us today, I could show you what could be done here. Don't you see we were fated to come to the sale today and…

"Hold on a moment…Are you suggesting that you, Chris Jenkins, who wouldn't change buses without thinking twice, are seriously considering, EVEN CONSIDERING the possibility of going back to that auction and buying this place."

"Why not? We have a little money put by and with my connections, I could get some great deals on everything. God knows I have owed enough favours. And at worst, we could always sell it on."

The pleading tone was in his voice again… and it looked as if no one has even considered it with all the other deals going on. It might be an ideal time.

"How much do you reckon it would cost?"

"Maybe seventy or eighty thousand."

"And we have that sort of money lying around with the money required to renovate it?"

"We could raise it if needed."

"Well,, you won't be happy knowing that you never tried but a top figure of eighty, no more."

"I love you Matty Jenkins."

"Let's stop messing about here, we have an auction to attend. And you owe me burger and chips."

Getting back as 1114 was sold at two hundred and twenty-three thousand, Chris signed in as a bidder and got a paddle.

"What is your number?"

"888."

"Isn't eight supposed to be lucky."

"We will soon see."

"Now ladies and gentlemen, item 1117. Where shall I start with this interesting project with potential, let's say twenty thousand, fifteen to get us going, any offers?"

Matty gently kicked Chris.

"Not yet, love," he whispered.

"Ten for the land," a voice shouted out.

"Well, it's a start, ten thousand pounds, and five hundred, thank you, eleven and a half, twelve, thirteen, thank you make no mistake there is no reserve on this property. Fourteen, thank you, fifteen at the side. Sixteen? No, then fifteen thousand pounds for the first time, fifteen thousand for the second time, at fifteen thousand for the third and final time. Sold 888 thank you, sir."

"It's ours!"

Three weeks later, the title deeds in their name arrived in the post.

"There you are Kevin, your mother and I are now property tycoons, land barons, Master and Mistress of the manse."

"What are you on about."

"There you are, we didn't want to say anything until it was all finalised but now, we can."

"Let's go and have a look then."

"Is this it?" said Kevin looking at the brambles birches and what looked like a pile of stones.

"Might be your birthright one day."

"Whoopee, can I go back to my womb now?" he said jokingly.

"You come and see it in three months when your mother and I have spent some time clearing the undergrowth."

"Uhh, where did the *your mother and I* come from?" said Matty.

"Three years did you say?" mocked Kevin.

"Don't forget I am off to Africa tomorrow and stay away from auctions." He laughed. "I will see you in three months."

Chris, now more determined than ever, bought a chain saw, with all the safety gear and a couple of thermos flasks. And soon he had the driveway cleared of over and undergrowth, leaving a large pile ready to burn. If he was really honest, he was enjoying the exercise. He was accompanied by Matty on many of the visits. Her main job being to keep the fire going and supply tea every now and then. They were occasionally joined by the estate greenkeeper who could chat for England but his manner was always pleasing and it gave Chris a rest now and then.

Now they were starting to see the outline of the building, they decided it was time to erect a boundary fence. So together with the estate owner's agent, they agreed to the boundary and arranged for a local contractor to put up a three-rail fence with a bottom rail and a rabbit protection wire. They discussed a set of pillars for the main gate but as the contractor pointed out it would be silly at this stage to limit the size of lorry that could enter and turn round. Having said that, Errol the contractor had taken away a day's work, but Matty and Chris let him do a day with them provided that everything was registered. The conservation officer and the archaeologists wanted to know what had been dug up and from where. They had taken photographs at every stage.

The house as it was, was bathed in glorious late afternoon sunshine, John Wardhay was standing in 'the kitchen garden' to be. Apart from being a part-time auctioneer, he was also one of the most innovative and clever architects for miles around.

"Be careful not to overdo the refurb and take away what years had achieved."

"We have no intention of spoiling anything John," Chris was indignant and hurt.

"No offence meant; I just feel that sometimes with older properties the original conception is to be admired. By the way do you have a name for the house?"

"Matty felt that the 'moon house' was too much like the American religious sect and conjures all kinds of myth and magic. Kevin came up with the best so far and that was *Half Moon House* on account of it not being completed yet."

"Sounds good to me. Do take care to try and find out how and why it was built this way and if you need my assistance, you know where I am."

"Great thanks, we are having an aerial picture taken next to see if any anomalies show up, a friend of mine is in the 'sealed knot society' and takes those kinds of pictures."

"Yes, it might just show up wells and drainage pits that a JCB digger might be too heavy for…"

"No big diggers here," said Matty, "restoring with love and care not to beat it into submission."

Thursday that week, photographs were on Chris's desk.

"John, it's Chris." The voice was excited and nervous. "Can you get over to my office? I've something to show you."

John arrived, puffed with the stairs, "I know I'm not fit as I was, what have you got to show me?"

"Look at these…"

"The old house from the air." John was dismissive.

"Yes, but look closer there and there…"

"Oh yes, either an underground tank or some sort of burial ground, and there appear to be two wells."

"So, what do you reckon?"

"I reckon tomorrow morning you and I are to be struck down with a tummy bug and I will meet you at the house around ten without arousing suspicion from our wives. I will bring a probe and see what we can unearth."

At the house, they marked out the areas carefully to avoid any caving in, after a short while using a spade found some brickwork. Chris's phone went off and it was Mark his assistant.

"It's just a tummy bug. I should be back tomorrow, look upon it as practice for when I retire, make some decisions."

John and Chris had made some real progress; they mapped out the wells and the apparent chambers John had the idea that they might be a large cistern for rainwater or some sort of sewage system maybe for a larger project, more likely to be the former. It was about time for the two of them to brave the walls of the building, chopping through huge but softwood elder bushes and silver birch trees, with ivy clinging on for dear life on the outside and through the various windows. Birds flew angrily out of every available orifice.

"God, I bet this place has a few tales to tell."

"It sure has," said a voice behind them.

John and Chris froze to the spot. Slowly, they turned to each other and to the door. There in the doorway with the aura of light around him stood a giant of a man poking at his pipe." "Sorry, did not mean to frighten you, but you were so intent on what you were doing."

Chris was the first to speak and whispered to John that he might need to get some new trousers. They both looked again to the door.

"Ex sergeant Jack Parker, I used to patrol this area 1910 to 1946. I was just passing and saw your vehicle. Old habits die hard."

"Do you remember what it was like?" Chris was always the one with direct questions. After all it was his job to get to the nitty-gritty of any situation.

"This old place was falling into rack and ruin even then, the locals reckoned it was haunted by the ghosts of John Henry and Hubert James."

"You don't seriously believe in ghosts of sixty years ago," said John scoffing at the very idea.

"Well, you two surely turned a little white a few minutes ago and the hairs on your necks are still rustling." He smiled.

"Look," said Chris, "I could do with a pint, why don't we take a break and nip to the pub, Jack can tell us a few more of his locally coloured tales. My shout of course."

Minutes later, John and Chris were enjoying a well-earned pint and Jack was about to earn his.

"When I came here in 1910 there was a bit of 'business' going on between John Henry and James Hubert Frimble who, it was reported, had fallen out with the local lothario gamekeeper, no one was ever sure why."

It was pure gossip but the two boys lost their father to pneumonia and pleurisy the year before and their mother it was said died of a broken heart the Two lads went back to the house after the funeral and although two gunshots were fired and two bodies were found at either end of the room, both shotguns in arms had recently been fired." He puffed his pipe.

"The coroner put it down to a tragic accident, if it was indeed murder who killed who first could never be established."

"What happened to the house?" asked John, going for another round.

"Well, they say and I was asked to investigate, that there were movements up there by candlelight and that's when all the talk of ghosts started. The cottage fell into disrepair and became overgrown. His Lordship had no desire to do anything with the place and it went downhill."

"But, do you remember how it came to be there in the first place?"

"I don't, but Young Josh down at the village, he may remember."

"Young Josh?"

"You'll find him on the granary steps 98. He is so… sometimes his mind plays funny tricks. Good luck with the renovations," and he was off to get a ploughman's lunch.

"What do you think?"

"Load of mumbo jumbo if you ask me and you just did."

But Chris knew he would have to visit this Young Josh.

Back at the cottage feeling refreshed, Chris was more determined than ever to follow up on the history of the house and also to write a complete journal of all activities in and around the house.

So began the Journal of Half Moon House, complete with photographs.

The roof timbers, although appearing sound, gave rise for concern, with a feeling they could collapse at any time, this being the general consensus. Internal scaffolding and acro bars were ordered to shore up the ceilings and roof.

With little else to do at this time, Chris utilised his surveying skills to begin the meticulous and laborious planning.

A week or so later, Chris, Matty, John and now Isabel, his reluctant and nervous wife who had been dragged into the mystique of anticipation, were discussing the plans over a drink or two.

Chris had drawn up the plans of the two-acre site from all the figures. "Now folks, are you ready for this?" He spread the plans out on the table and weighted it down at the corners.

"Wow, it looks like a helicopter," said Isabel in all innocence.

"I suppose it does really, but look closer, it resembles a Celtic cross."

"Oh, yes."

"And another thing, the drive runs exactly North to South."

"So, you are saying this pile of stones may have been designed more carefully than we thought."

"Precisely, I think I need to speak to this Young Josh, and see if he can throw any light on it all."

Chris drove down to Melfort the next morning and an excited John soon found the steps but no Josh. The steps were very crude with side wings to protect the workers who would have carried bags of milled flour from wind blowing dust into their eyes. They were also an ideal spot for the pipe smokers taking a break from milling. They could imagine two of the workers swapping stories of the day before going back to the world of sign language in the noisy mill.

They sat there looking out into the countryside imagining the men in the fields with busy scythes cutting the corn or the hay and the wives with their children bringing in freshly brewed ales in flagons and freshly baked pasties.

Chris was about to sink his teeth onto a golden-brown three-cornered pasty when he heard a gruff voice.

"Oi, that's my dreaming seat, I'll have you know."

"I'm sorry?" questioned Chris.

"That's where I spend most of my days now, waiting for my time to come for the great reaper in the sky." The gruff voice went on.

"Ah, you must be Young Josh," said Chris.

"Mr Joshua Young to all but my friends and as I don't know you from Adam."

"I do apologise Mr Young, Jack Parker told me we could find you here and he called you Young Josh."

"Well, he's no friend of mine either, the name has sort of stuck from when I was at school."

"Can I please introduce myself; I am Chris Jenkins and this is my friend John Wardhay. My wife, Matty and myself have bought the old woodland house on the Pressguard estate, where I believe you worked for a while."

"I did that. Man and boy."

"Great, If you have the time perhaps, I could ask you a few questions about the house and its history.

"Oh, I got the time alright but the memory ain't what it was, mind I find a half pint or two does help."

"Good idea, shall we?"

In front of a blazing fire and a couple of half pints, Chris put his tape recorder on and began.

"When did you become gamekeeper on the estate?"

"I came here in 1892 after my 21st birthday, as underkeeper to a man called Allsopp. When he retired, I took over."

"I was not married and lodged with the Allsopps and when he retired, they stayed on to look after me."

"So, did you remember the woodland folly being built?"

"Oh yes, it was the talk of the village how old man Frimble managed to get the land and permission to build the Folly. Derek Frimble used to do most of the legal work for Lord Pressguard and rumour has it that they used to play cards on a regular basis for money like you know bridge and poker mostly." The wrinkled old man with a twinkle in his eye sipped from the near empty glass Chris motioned to John who took the hint and went to the bar.

"There was this one night that I think a considerable amount of whisky was consumed and things got a little bit out of hand. Derek apparently was well down on the evening's stakes and lodged his wife's personal services for a weekend to cover his bet."

Fortunately, they were playing three card brag and His Lordship put down two aces and a queen, a winning hand by most standards but Derek had the other two aces and a King. That was close. His Lordship, being quite taken by the idea of a weekend in the company of Melinda Frimble, offered Derek a plot of land and permission to build on it in exchange."

"What for a couple of nights in the hay," said Chris.

"You never saw the lady," said Josh. "She was an absolutely stunning woman, a real cracker by any standards."

"So, he agreed and his wife did not object."

"Well rumour has it that she quite fancied the opportunity to live an aristocratic lifestyle with the idle rich for a weekend. Apparently she had several weekends of 'luxury'."

"This happened before my time but folk around do say or did, because the majority of that era are dead now. That Derek tried to atone for his behaviour in treating his wife that way by designing a house in a shape to appease the gods in other words…

"In the shape of a Celtic cross."

"Ah, not many people had noticed that."

"We did an aerial survey and a ground plan which would confirm that."

"He apparently intended to build a house in the round the first part As Is that was for him and his wife Mary and then as they had children he would add on and for his children's children etc.

Hoping there would be enough room so that as one generation died out another would take on part of the house, It was to be an eternal circle of life"

"Let me get you another drink."

"Perhaps, a small whisky to follow will stop the wind from blowing up my kilt on those steps."

"You know," continued Josh, "I haven't thought that hard for a long time."

"Jack was saying there were two sons when he came here."

"Aye, they were born within a year of each other and tragically they were both found dead on Ambleside Hoe. Eighteen they were."

"Jack said they had possibly killed each other, but no proof."

"Well, thereby another story was told but that will have to wait for another day."

"Were there no other children?"

"Rumour has it that yes Mary did have another child—a daughter but that she died very soon after birth funny that because she was born alive, and yet no formal burial." He dropped his voice and looked around to see who was in the bar and whispered, "The baby was born nine months after THE weekend if you follow my drift with no grave and no funeral, the ghost is supposed to 'aunt the 'ouse."

A cold chill went down Chris's spine.

"Do you know what the chambers are underground?" asked Chris.

"Do you mean the sewage pits, like the ones built in London, Derek was well up on modern drainage and had two cisterns built to take waste one from either end so that they were isolated from either family."

"I see and the two wells?"

"Only knew of one in the middle of the circle for all to share."

"Definitely another on the outside."

"Don't know about that, it's a pity Charlie Evans isn't still alive he would have dug it, by the way if you dig into the surface, you will find foundations for the whole circle and the arms of the cross."

"So, the foundations are still there for the full moon then."

"Full moon, what are you talking about, don't believe all the rumours you hear." Chris noticed a distinct change of voice and tone, he bought Josh another drink and left him to his own devices for another day. Josh seemed quite morose for some unknown reason. "He gets like that at times," said the barman, "take no notice, he will be as right as rain tomorrow."

Chris could not help himself going back to the house and was quite pleased that the scaffolding poles and clips and the acro bars were here as well. As he walked around, he could not help but wonder what exactly had happened here, is there more to it all or was he imagining things.

He watched as the sun set and went home.

The erection of scaffolding was supervised by another work colleague Pete, a scaffolder before becoming a safety inspector on the council and it was soon looking ship-shape. Pete could only do the day but showed Chris and John the basics. "If we get it all up, could you come back and check it for us?"

"When you think you are finished, give me a ring and I will arrange a 'safety check' from the council.

With that the pick-up sped off down the track.

"Look I have ten days holiday due how about I come and give you a hand to get this scaffold up."

"Will Isobel mind?"

"No, she will probably come over herself because she loves to be hands-on."

A week later, John joined with Chris and they began scaffolding the inside like professionals until mid-afternoon, John called to Chris to be careful where he trod as a small hole had appeared in the floor. As Chris, intrepid as ever, walked over to John the floor gave way beneath him. Amidst all the dust and stoney grit, there was some kind of tunnel.

"Are you alright, John."

"Yes, you?"

"Yes, it seems like some kind of tunnel but not very deep."

"But look, John. This is scary, if you look over there you can see some stone steps leading to the house wall."

"What the…it does not make sense."

"I know what you are thinking, where?"

"More like 'Who'," said John.

"There is a torch in the car we had better not have a naked light here you never know what gasses have built up, I will go and get it."

"Err not without me, thank you," and they both went together.

Bravely brandishing the torch and smashing away at cobwebs with a brush from the car, they looked for the steps. Why are there always cobwebs when there are no flies.

The tunnel seemed to slope away from them and there was the bottom of some steps leading up into some sort of void or darkened room or one without windows.

"Chris!!!" John grasped Chris's arm, they both froze as the torch was dancing on a shining white skeleton sitting in the corner of the dark room.

Seconds seemed like hours…John was the first to speak. "Let's get the hell out of here."

They carefully backtracked and were so pleased to see daylight. "What the ******* hell do we do now?"

John sounded very frightened when he said, "Are you sure that you saw what I saw?"

"No, but I think it was and I am certain that I am surely not going to make certain."

"Shall we call the police?"

"Yes, but I don't see the need to rush."

At which point the shock turned into laughter.

"I'll get my mobile."

Ten minutes later blue lights flashing and sirens blazing, a squad car arrived with two burly policemen and asked what the problem was.

When told that they thought there was a dead body or rather skeleton in a tunnel under the house, the burly policemen started to shrink to a normal size, "Have you two been drinking?"

Then, "Are you sure this is not a hoax?"

"There is a torch there, go and take a look for yourself."

"Hmm, very well, you two stay here and I will get a task force out here...

Now can I have your names and addresses? and why are you here?"

"Because I am the new owner, and together we were working on making the scaffolding safe."

"I see," said the most forward of the policemen who seemed to be starting his own murder inquiry, "And do you often work together as it were, sir?"

"What are you implying, Constable?"

"Just collecting facts, sir."

Thankfully there were no more questions as two more squad cars and a minibus arrived.

"These two claimed to have found a body inside a tunnel in this building, sir, Mr Chris Jenkins and Mr John Wardhay."

"Yes, thank you, Constable Jones, now where is the body?"

"At the end of this little tunnel are some steps leading to a room. Here is a torch if you would like to take a look."

"Is it safe down there, Mr Jenkins?"

"We are not sure."

"Right lads, safety gear on and then go down and take a look."

Two constables donned white overalls and pit helmets with lamps and went in.

Emerging covered in dust they had established that yes indeed there were skeletal remains of a body in a sitting position in the corner of a room.

"Right, get a forensic team down here, constable Jones, let's have the scene cordoned off and set up the minibus as an incident room.

Now you two, play is over for today so perhaps you could accompany me to the minibus."

"Mr Jenkins, perhaps you could tell us more"

"Nothing to tell really, Inspector, my wife and I bought this place at auction a couple of months ago from the Pressguard estate, we have been working on it at odd times since then. My friend John Wardhay has been here to help. We were shoring the roof up to make it safe when part of the floor gave way and you know the rest.

"I see, do you have the deeds to this place and do we know who the previous occupants were?

The deeds are at the solicitor's office and as far as we know no-one has lived here for the last forty years. Someone called Frimble, we believe, lived here at that time.

Well sorry to inconvenience you but I think I shall go and see the scene myself. Could you remain here please.

An hour later the forensic team had allowed the remains to be taken to the laboratory for examination but did not suspect foul play.

"Please leave everything as it is for the moment until we have completed our investigations."

Matty and Isobel were fascinated and could hardly wait while the two men had a shower to rid themselves of the dirt and dust.

"What do we do now?" asked Matty.

"We wait to see what the police have to say."

The wait was not long, the next morning just after breakfast, the Inspector arrived.

"Please, don't be alarmed."

"Mr. Jenkins, you will be pleased to know that no murder has been committed the body has been there sometime but it would appear there was no foul play and death occurred by natural causes approximately forty years ago.

"Where does that leave us."

The coroner has been informed of an unknown body having been found in some dubious circumstances. But indeed, it was a woman, will be recorded as natural causes. Which means that the body such as it is, can be released for burial in your good hands or alternatively the bones can be kept for forensic scientific research.

"I would think the latter please."

"I will have the paperwork sent over to you. So, thank you and good day, my team will have left the scene by the end of the day. Thank you for your cooperation. If you have any more 'finds' that we should know about please let us know."

The four of them went back to the house not knowing what to do or where to start.

"We are not giving in," said Chris.

"There appears to be an anomaly here in the wall, look, there is a wall beyond this with a ceiling above, it is weird that there appears to be no natural light."

After searching in the thickly embedded ivy John eventually found an opening of sorts, he was going to put his hand in but thought better of that and poked a stick through. The stick was not hurt so he and Chris cut back the ivy to find a rotten window frame of about 30cms wide and 60cms deep just wide enough to get the torch inside.

"Wow," said Matty, "I can see a table, chair, what looks like the remains of a bed or bedlinen, a few bits of crockery and some sort of machine on the table. And in the corner is a pile of brown paper."

Chris had had enough and determined to get to the bottom of any mystery he ripped the window frame out and a few loose bricks to make the hole big enough to climb through. The machine turned out to be what looked like an early typewriter but as soon as they touched the pile of brown paper it turned to dust.

They each had the same feeling that they were intruding on someone's life of loneliness and solitude. Chris spotted a candle holder on the wall with a large stalagmite of wax below it.

"Look at this." There was a mirror all spotted and pockmarked. Behind it was a small door, obviously the way out. so having found a way in they all wondered what else they would find.

"Let's take this, what seems to be a very early typewriter back home and clean it up. It could be worth a bob or two. ``Matty, ever the pragmatic one, "It will give us time to think.

Surprisingly the typewriter was in remarkable order even though the type ribbon was intact. and it was a Remington which they found dated 1895 checked because of the serial number.

"Chris, do you have any A4 paper?"

"It won't work," he scoffed. "Here a whole 500 sheets, enjoy," he said laughing.

Matty put a piece of paper into the machine and turned the wheel handle at the side and the paper came up in front of her and she tested a key, immediately with her hands held above the machine it started to move quite slowly and deliberately. Her fingers were moving the keys involuntarily and the machine was clattering.

"Come on Issie, we've had enough laughs for today you can stop now."

But Isobel was not looking at or hearing anyone, in a trance-like state with her fingers hitting the keys, the paper turned up automatically.

Chris was standing at the back of Issie and grasped her hands from the machine bringing her out of what seemed some sort of trance.

"What the…"

Look, said Chris, he carefully pulled the paper out of the machine, it appeared blank but when he held it up to the light clearly words could be seen imprinted onto the paper.

*'My name is Megan Frimble this is a chronicle of woodland folly I live with my mother Mary and my father*

*Derek I have two brothers John and Hubert I have written these to tell the world of the injustices that the people of melfort have imposed on us.*

"My God what have we found?" said Chris feeling a cold draught up his back.

"Shouldn't we tell the police?" said Matty

"Tell them what exactly, I was here and I don't believe what just happened."

"She wants me to continue."

"WHO?"

"Megan."

"Aw, come on Issie, this is beginning to scare me."

"There is nothing to fear, I know it."

"I am not so sure," said John.

"I will try," said Matty.

"Just a minute, I have some carbon paper here, if we put a piece between two sheets it will print onto the other piece and will be easy to read." He slowly rolled the paper into the machine. Matty sat in front of it and held her hands over the keys. Nothing happened. She tried touching the keys, but nothing happened.

"Let me try John," said Isobel, "if she wanted to hurt anyone it would have attacked by now."

So, Issie took up her place in front of the machine. As she dangled her hand over the keys her face changed and the fingers started to hit what appeared to be random keys.

Clitter clatter the machine began and then speeded up Matty gripped Chris's arm and John was visibly going paler and paler.

"Chris," whispered John, "Do you have any of that aerosol easing oil."

"Over by the window."

John slipped away and came back with the can ready for action. He sprayed the central area of the typewriter and the noise decreased dramatically. It was then he noticed that the fingers were not actually touching the keyboard at all.

"What do we do now," asked Chris.

"Read it," said Issie, smiling.

"Are you feeling okay, only you seem to be far away."

"Just a nap that's all."

"You did some more typing."

"Did I, what does it say?"

"No one has looked yet."

"Well get looking then."

Chris unrolled the papers and sure enough there was a blue copy.lm sitting here in my lifelong prison chamber with only the night time for company. my mother used to visit me but has stopped now. I believe she has died. my brothers stole this machine and my mother taught me how to use it I can never leave this chamber in the day because i have the devils mark on my face and chest at night i can walk freely but it frightens me.

Silence fell over the Four, broken by Chris;

"What in the world do we do now?"

"This is giving me the creeps," said Matty

"There is nothing to fear," said Isobel. "At least I don't feel any fear at all."

"Let's do a bit of research if we can first." John was certainly worried.

They all agreed, Matty was to see the local vicar, John was to see the curator at Brewald town hall museum to get the lowdown on the typewriter Chris and Isobel would go and see Young Josh again.

Chris felt strange as he drove up the Melfort Road and Issie went quiet as they passed the end of the lane.

"My eyes are smarting" she said as they got into Melfort "Have you any sunglasses in the car?"

"In the glove compartment "

"Thanks that's better she said, slipping them on, must be the watery sunlight ".

In the distance Chris saw Josh sitting on the steps and pulled over. As they walked up to him calmly chuffing at his pipe obviously oblivious to the world at large he instantly changed, looked worried and paled "What are you doing here?"

"We 've come to see you again to talk about old times just like the other day," said Chris, quite concerned at the change of tone.

"Not Wi' 'er, the hussie, take 'er away from me." with that he spat on the floor and scurried away. Isobel was visibly shocked.

"Jack did say he could be a bit weird said Chris, "Come on you need a brandy."

"Frightened I would say, I wonder what he has to hide."

"He can be a bit funny at times, gets lost in his own world" that was the barmans excuse for him when the tale was related to him. "He is over ninety after all, won't go out after dark and always has his pocket bible with him." Handing over the drinks. "If I get to that age without going doolally then I will be well pleased," with that he was off to the other end of the bar.

Matty had decided that a very old friend of her mother's might possibly be called in to help with the dilemma. He had been the local vicar but he knew very little of the story, mostly titbits of gossip and no accounting for any of them, People hearing strange howling at night while out walking their dogs or hearing the screams of a 'tortured soul' coming from the woods, some courting couples say they had clothes and monies stolen as were some houses in the district. Oh and horses apparently let out of locked stables to end up on the common. none of which were ever really substantiated.

There were tales of well water turning green overnight, windows smashed at night even some spectres seen in the wood. Notes in the vestry tell of frightened congregations filling the church on a Sunday, 'standing in the aisle' and all sorts of occult tales and body snatching.

"Err, thank you, Vicar, I think."

"The strangest thing was that stories continued during the two war periods and long before and after the two brother's incident. There were several 'seances held in the district and again according to vestry notes the vicar was asked to exorcise two cottages at the edge of the village. Nothing ever happened in the village centre and in those days there was no street lighting.

"Do you believe in ghosts Mr Mumford?" asked Matty.

"Strange question to ask a vicar in light of our conversation. Is there something you would like to tell me about?"

"Well yes but first I need you to tell me about your feelings concerning Ghosts?"

"Ah that old chestnut, If I'm honest with myself and God I have to say that I don't believe in ghostly apparitions that float around in the day or night. But I strongly believe there may be forces beyond our normal parameters which may never be explained. Does that help. "

"Yes" she went on to relate the happenings of the last day or two.

"Ah I had heard the police had been called to Folly Cottage "

But the weirdest thing of all, she told him of the typewriter.

He instantly crossed himself and went quiet for a moment or two. "Do you know what the stories are?"

"Not yet, we have been a little concerned that we are meddling in things we don't understand."

"Quite so, but in my humble experience if a 'poltergeist is at work then things are quite often destroyed or thrown around in temper by whatever force." He thought for a moment. "If, on the other hand there is a restless spirit in need of solace and comfort then it would be my duty to help if I can. I shall ask the bishop for his guidance, In the meantime you must follow your own consciences."

John had been to the museum curator and found out that the typewriter was a Remington made at the time when typeface had either capitals and small case letters but it was well known to go wrong and just type in one or the other. he dated it around the turn of the century and said if repaired would be sort after by collectors. He suggested that if he brought it into the museum, they could probably trace who the original owner was because of the serial number on it. Back in Melfort Chris and Isobel had finished their drinks and were on their way home, Isobel had the notion of stopping at the cottage as it was on the way home.

There they went directly to the tarpaulin covered room, opened it up to reveal a crumbling table, chair and bed with a pile of what looked like old rotted bedding material or possibly clothing of some kind. There were odd bits of collars and buttons still evident in the pile.

"I am just going to look in the tunnel again to see if there is an end to it "

"Be careful Chris "

"I won't be long."

Chris came back after a few minutes "I've found the end, near the end is a second set of steps leading" …. He stopped. "Issie, Isobel, where are you ?".

"Looking for me?"

He reeled round to find Issie draped in a white shawl and nothing else!!

"Isobel?" he said in a quiet voice and rubbing his eyes.

"You mistake me sir," the figure in white spoke, "My name is Megan."

"Now come on Isobel, a joke is a joke but this is going too far," said Chris, feeling the hair rising on the back of his neck and a cold waft of air blasting through his body. Isobel apparently fainted in front of him and he bent down to pick her up. As he grasped the shawl wrapped body her clothes reappeared and Isobel was in his arms.

"Where am I, what am I doing down here?"

Not wishing to worry her he said, you fainted or tripped.

"Let's go home, Chris."

"Yes let's." The bemused Chris was almost silent on the way home. It was a good job Issie had said she had a headache and welcomed the quiet ride.

"You are quiet, dear," said Matty.

"Just trying to assimilate the information of the day that is all."

How do you tell your wife and best friend that his wife had just appeared almost naked in front of him and she apparently did not remember anything of the visit. Either he had been daydreaming when these strange happenings occurred. So why was he dreaming about another woman and a friend's wife or the whole thing was a hallucination and he would awake in a cold sweat at any moment.

Back home and with a couple of drinks inside them Isobel started the ball rolling "Come on, where's your spirit of adventure let's have another try with the typewriter.

"Do you really think we should" asked John.

"We will never get to the bottom of it otherwise "she winked at Chris.

They put the typewriter complete with the loaded paper on the table in front of her, she held her hands out like a professional piano player and cracked her knuckles and held her hands above the keys. Nothing happened at first then Issie touched one of the keys and with her eyes fully closed began typing tip tip tap steadily down the page, John readied another two pages with carbon between and by the time he was ready she had reached the bottom of the page and the papers spilled out. Issie stopped until the new pages were in place and began again. About three quarters down the page, she stopped. opened her eyes, her hands went floppy on the machine, "Has anything happened "

"You mean you are not aware that you have just typed two pages"

"Let's read them then."

Matty read :-


*Why is that I am so forlorn and why do I have to carry the burden of guilt to eternity. It is none of my doing that my mother went with his lordship to please my father and produced me as a child of the devil with this mark on my face and Bosom that cannot see day or the eyes of a man.*

*Why am I left to rot in this place and die without child, fed on my own and not seen by my brothers lest they be cursed for my mother's deed. My father should be the one with the evil Lord to be shamed allowing the fates to produce me. They are cursed to eternal damnation, one as a dust laden well digger and the other by the pox banished to not return not even as a fly.*

*I cannot rest until the sins of these parts have been aired to rid myself of guilt bestowed upon me. I praise the lord that my mother gave me sustenance as a child and taught me to read and write like a lady, she has been absolved and has passed to the other side but the vicar and the gamekeeper will not pass through unless they beg forgiveness for their deeds and evil exploits with women and each other.*


"My Goodness what have we opened up?" said John.

"Something we cannot stop now," said Isobel.

Chris, remembering his vision of the day, suggested they sleep on it and tomorrow decide what we should do and where this might take us.

Isobel slept soundly that night or at least thought she did. John dreamt about the mountain of paper spewing forth from the typewriter, not knowing how or when it would stop. Matty awoke to the sounds of Mr Mumford and his sermon about meddling with things we knew nothing about.

Chris sank into a deep sleep and awoke to find Isobel once more leading him into the chamber, unable to stop this vision of firm pink flesh in a flimsy covering revealing her long legs as she floated into the bed chamber. As she floated, the wind ripped her covering from her revealing a huge red birthmark on her neck to her midriff. He turned away but she cupped his hands on her and prevented him from escaping. He awoke screaming with Matty at his side "It's okay, only a dream."

It had been only minutes into his sleep but felt like hours and he had never felt like this before.

At breakfast, the four of them who quite often would have gone on to play a round of golf were discussing dreams with Chris nearly choking on his toast.

He thought about 'coming clean' with his dream but then thought better of it.

"Are we going to continue with the letters today?" said Isobel, eagerly anticipating the danger and excitement.

"I think we should give them a rest for today ," said Chris "And do something constructive at the house John how about you and I carry on with the scaffolding and you two could.

"Explore the tunnel," said Isobel, all excited.

"Chris."

"Yes, John?"

"Something, I have been meaning to ask, what do you intend to do with the house once we have finished if we ever do."

"Not sure actually, any particular reason for asking?"

"Well Issie and I have been talking and we wondered if you might consider that there would be enough room for two accommodations and whether you might consider taking on board a couple of willing partners on the project?"

"Even with all its problems?"

"Yes," they spoke as one person, "they are opportunities not problems."

"What do you think, Matty?"

"Sounds like an excellent idea after all we are such good friends anyway."

"Alright, I will have the papers drawn up next week."

The two men really sweated with a vengeance that day and had the rest of the scaffolding up inside the house. Now they could start to clear out the flora inside the house. The two girls resplendent in their boiler suits and complete with torches had found nothing except spiders and webs in the tunnel. The well section had circular steps on the inside wall. It appeared dry but with no handrail of any kind they thought better of climbing down. The collapsed tunnel they thought might make a feature if it was cleared and re-walled giving a unique sunken walkway, but that would be up for discussion much later.

Neither of the pairs had entered the little room that day even though tempted and, on the way, home picked up a take-away. Bunging it in the oven while they showered and changed.

John and Isobel were quite used to staying over, especially after a drink session or the like Chris, ever the gentleman, waited quietly while the others showered and changed. While he was waiting, he set the table for the supper and arranged the drinks. As he was putting out the mats there was a shout from the stairs and Isobel was leaning over the banister rail and yelled that there was a bottle in her basket that needed chilling. as he looked up at Isobel in the flimsy shower robe he was reminded of the days and the previous night's occurrences, She hurried away oblivious of any thoughts he might have, His thoughts not so easy to quench and he certainly had the shower setting at a much lower temperature than normal.

They celebrated a successful day and a future partnership "Let's explore with the Ouija board."

The ever-adventurous Isobel was always up for a laugh.

"Before we do," said Matty "Let's explore what we have. If we are to take any of it seriously or consider it is some kind of enormous hoax."

So, we are told that in order to build and purchase the property there was some sort of tryst between the two heavy gamblers the then Lord Pressguard and Derek Frimble. If What we are told here is right somehow Megan's mother was procured and the liaison produced Megan.

"But Josh said the child had died at birth and it would have not been procurement because she was a willing participant. "Megan calls herself a child of the devil in the letters with some sort of birthmark," said John.

"A huge birthmark from her forehead to her midriff," muttered Chris.

All the other three said simultaneously, "How could you know that?"

"Err, I saw a picture of the great lord himself somewhere during the sale and it depicted him with this huge strawberry mark. I just deducted that this was a hereditary birthmark," Chris was definitely colouring up and sweating.

"Is there something you are not telling us?" asked Matty.

"No, I don't think so."

"Well, a mark like that would certainly have been hereditary and if the mark was on the baby, it would explain the disappearance of the baby at birth to avoid embarrassment to his lordship and Megan's mother."

"Do you mean that she could have been kept secret for all of her life just being cared for by her mother in that dungeon cell?" exclaimed Isobel.

How Archaic and the stone building was a sham! Matty turned to Isobel. I think we may have to use your services and possibly the vicars to placate this Megan if we are to live in harmony in this house.

"I don't mind, ready when you are!"

"Look, tomorrow night when the lads are at snooker, we will have another session and see what transpires. I will get some more carbon paper as I can see we will be needing quite a lot.

Chris hardly dared to go to sleep that night but must have done because the alarm woke him.

"Are you sure you can handle this on your own tonight, we could always cancel the snooker."

"Look, she has not hurt anyone in this and Issie seems totally unaffected by it. I can phone you if required."

"Promise you will.'

"Oh alright."

That evening John picked up Chris and off they went, Issie and Matty decided a drink first would probably loosen things up a bit as it might be a long night.

Isobel made herself comfortable in the armchair in front of the machine and Matty was at her side to feed the paper.

"Are we ready then, Let's begin."

Bang on the stroke of eleven the two lads came in with the girls still at the machine, with Issie still holding station above the keys and Matty feeding the paper like an automaton.

Matty motioned them to be quiet and they stood transfixed as the paper fell from the roller and Matty gently lifted Issy's fingers clear of the keys.

Isobel Yawned. "Hello lovers. Is it that time already, how are we doing Matty."

"It's fantastic, I've never heard of such a thing happening, there are thirty pages of highly incriminating stuff here, if the people are still alive." she paused, "and I have a feeling there are more to come."

"How do you mean?" said Chris.

"Each one of these stories is either a made-up fiction from a very knowledgeable and fertile mind or a graphic recollection of real-life occurrences."

"If we are to believe all this...," said John, still with scepticism in his voice, "then they must be true because Megan would have little or no comprehension of life's happenings to fall back on. She had no books in the room and she had been isolated from general society."

"That's right, Chris shall we get started reading them?"

Matty thought for a moment, "I think not until we have them all, then we can follow more closely the mind set patterns and if we prejudge, we may lose the link through Issie.

"Tomorrow we will try again if you are okay with that Issie?"

"Perhaps we should all get a decent night's sleep first,: observed John.

"I'm fine about it, I just seem to be some sort of intermediary in all this with no effect on me."

"A catalyst, dear," corrected John.

"Great. Tomorrow it is then and I will get these copied down at the library so that we all have a copy to refer to."

During the night, Matty had the most vivid dreams of her life with faces she had never seen before, and situations in places she had not been in yet so real she was frightened to move.

When she awoke, she was confronted by a circle of people all with a paper sheet in front of them going round and round, she was sat on the bed in the middle of the room, Chris was at the bottom of the bed unable it would appear to be woken with a whispering chant that started to get louder and louder until she had to press her hands over her ears to stop the noise.

Chris awoke and found her sitting on the edge of the bed with a glazed look and her hands over her ears. He stroked her arm gently, "Come on back to bed, dear it was only a dream."

He led her back to the pillow and put her back under the covers with a little peck on the cheek, she was back to sleep in seconds.

In the morning she could not remember anything suspicious but as the day went on little flashbacks that she could not understand plagued her.

At the library she paid for the copier machine and tried to print the typed letters. The machine struck up then stopped when it came to following the page. She tried again and the same thing happened. She called the librarian over who tried three times even with her own Mastercard but the machine refused to go across the page. The assistant then fetched the book she was reading and tried to copy a page. absolutely perfect no problem So Matty tried again and the machine would not copy that paper.

"It must be something to do with the paper although I can't think why. Matty accepted the refund intending to go somewhere else but her thoughts went back to her dream and she felt a great impulse to go home.

When she arrived the back door was open and Matty could hear a tap tap tap in the front room she thought, picking up the mop which was the closest thing to hand she crept round the door,

Isobel was sitting at the typewriter with just a flimsy white see through shawl sitting at the typewriter with her hands over the keys which were going quicker than Matty had seen before.

Matty froze at first thinking perhaps she was in a dream and she should not startle her but after a while any fears of harm were diminishing fast, she had after all seen Issie typing before, but she had not seen the shawl before and why had she no clothes on under the shawl. Slowly, coming back to her senses Matty backed up to close the door and stop the howling draught which would give her pneumonia she thought. Isobel was still transfixed to the table and putting her own paper into the carriage.

Isobel spun round on her chair and said "Done" in a strangely quiet voice, not her usual brash tone.

Matty went slowly but surely to the other room to get a coat or something to throw over Issie's shoulder but when she turned back to the room Isobel was fully dressed, shaking her head somewhat she said, "Am I dreaming? Matty, what are you going to do with that mop? Hey, this is not our house it is yours. What am I doing here?"

"Hence the mop, when I came back the door was wide open and I found you here."

"What is that?" she was looking at a fan shaped pile of dust at least five millimetres thick on the floor.

"I can't be certain," said Matty, "But you remember the white shawl you and Chris found at the house the other day,"

"The one Chris wouldn't touch for some reason."

"Yes…" said Matty, "where is it?"

"My …. The last thing I remember was picking it up and putting it around my shoulders thinking it was musty and cold."

"Sit down, Isobel," ordered Matty.

"When I came in a while ago… you are not going to believe this… I found you sitting at the typewriter typing and feeding paper yourself to the machine… with not a stitch on apart from the shawl."

"You are kidding."

"Wish I was," said Matty.

"Then what happened?"

"After a few minutes you said done, and pointed to the door. By the time I had spun round and back again the shawl was on the floor and you were in ordinary clothes again. Almost like one of those joke pens that show a lady naked and when you turn the pen right-side up, she is fully clothed."

"Eh, this is real ghoulish stuff."

"That is where the shawl floated to and landed."

"Wow." They both backed out into the kitchen, it seemed more sinister now there were two in on the secret and with Matty telling Issie what happened at the library.

Chris dashed home after getting a message from Matty and John had a similar call, they almost arrived identically.

"What's up doc," joked John.

"Not sure I only just arrived, but I think it is serious."

They found Matty and Isobel staring into coffee cups with Matty motioning to the dining room.

As they entered the dining room a cloud of white dust blew up and an arctic blast of air hit the doorway. Chris tried to shut the door but it was wrenched from his hand. The cloud of dust gathered and flew past them into the passage and out through the open door. There was a flurry of white papers floating back to the floor having been lifted by the backdraft of the blast.

"OH GOD LOOK," said Matty the pages were apart but joined and read HELP on the table top.

Calm was restored and everything with the exception of the paper was in exactly the same place as before. No one spoke for several minutes. Isobel broke the eerie silence.

"Now that wasn't fun."

Matty was about to let out a big scream when a last piece of paper fell from the ceiling onto Isobel's feet. Picking it up and holding it to the light. Thank you could be clearly read in the light.

That seemed to break the darkness of the situation, Things did not seem so ominous anymore.

And they began talking like gibbering wrecks.

"We are going to need help, but we need to go through these papers to see if there are any stories we can tell" said Matty with glee in her voice.

"Shouldn't we involve the vicar in all this?" asked Chris.

"No, don't you remember in the first part of the story he was involved in some way.

"But that won't be the present vicar or gamekeeper surely, they will not have known Derek Frimble or his family ".

"No but what about Josh and Jack and perhaps the old vicar has been put out to grass somewhere in one of those theological homes ".

"Be careful what we say and do, we can't just go throwing accusations like this around.

"Right Boss what do we do now?" Isobel was in her impish mood.

"First, I think we should try to read these scripts, how did you get on with the copying Matty?"

Of course, Matty had to tell them all about the library machine.

"Is this Megan not making life too easy for us?" said John.

"We will have to share what we have, look, the other 'new' ones are just plain paper."

"Do you feel anything?" said John laughing. "I think I'm getting into the spirit of it."

"Can we be just a little serious," said Chris. "Right if you are sure, you are up to it, Issie."

She sat at the chair and arms out and nothing, the two blokes went out of the room and still nothing but when they re-entered there was a breeze and a single piece of paper went to the floor, on close inspection they could see the word amen indented in handwriting not type.

The room went very quiet and a solemn mood overtook them.

*I am not sure how much more the old ticker can stand,* was the thought on John's mind.

Matty and Issie picked up the papers and led the way to the kitchen table.

Chris found a soft pencil and began lightly pencilling over the paper.

"It's not easy to make sense of these, it looks like some night time excursions were made on a regular basis over quite a period of time. He said, reading one of them. the moon is high tonight and went over to the ramble path and hid behind the old oak there just before the bend where a policeman met another policeman and handed him four fesants. Later, I watched Bob and Charlie come out of the woods with fesants over their shoulders there was a shot and I ran back to the house the next night I saw two men put something bag into a hole near the tree and filled it over, with leaves I went back two days later I found a bottle and opened it, there was an awful smell and I will keep away from it. But I took the flask of awful liquid and put it in the wall.

There is another, Isobel.

The moon is bright and the stars are out aplenty, went to the edge of the cliff where a white pony stood with a saddle on it. A man was lying with a woman and they were groaning and screaming I watched the man put something in his trousers he was swearing at the woman and kicked her, she stood up and he pushed her over the cliff there was a long scream and then nothing.

The man Robert ran the white pony to the edge of the cliff and he stopped while the pony thundered over the cliff. I have his riding crop in the wall.

"We are going to need to do some serious investigating into these stories," said Chris. "Listen to this one."

*I am now in my nineteenth year and bleed regularly as my mother said I would but I stopped after the time Josh found me watching badgers in the wood and while I was waiting I had to pee josh grabbed me from behind pushed my dress over my head and put something inside me It were josh and I took his watch from his chain it is in the wall.*

"Wow," said Matty this must be a follow on from that: *I'm in my nineteenth year and the baby makes it not easy to get around. I find rabbits and hares hanging on my fence so Josh is helping, I will take it to him now he is born. I watched Josh and his wife look around to see who had left him but I hid.*

"I think I need that drink now," said Isobel.

"I think we all do," said Chris.

No wait, Matty was looking at the paper intensely.

Listen to this.

*After the wind and the rain, we have had the woodmen have been out cutting trees for the winter f but dad has been brought home lying on something I can hear mum crying I want to go to her but the lads will see me and be cursed later mum brought me food and told me dad was dead and he would be buried in the churchyard tomorrow but I must not be seen. that next day there was drinking and dancing in the garden. mum was drunk and three men the vicar, Charlie Evans and that josh egged her on to dance naked for them and they all entered her and crept away like thieves in the night leaving my mum on the floor asleep. I stole the vicar's bible and hid that in the wall.*

"I wonder if we can put these into some sort of chronological order," Matty was thinking.

"It will take ages just to read them, never mind filing them," said John.

"I think we have read enough for tonight. Did someone mention a drink.?

They had certainly tucked away a few pints of home brew and a fair amount of tonic with as much gin in it but nothing seemed to dull the intrigue that these stories were evoking. Someone had opened the box and they all had to come out!

"Oh, what the heck we will not sleep yet anyway let's read some more of these lurid stories about this Megan Frimble and the evil characters of the day," said Matty.

"We ought to be going home," said John.

"Simple enough, stay the night." Matty was certainly slurring.

"That's the best offer I've had in a long time," said John.

"Naughty naughty, we have enough of those innuendos in these stories without you adding to them. She laughed.

Chris however coloured up at the thought of his dreams, that dress or lack of it and the proximity. "Right," he said changing the subject quickly. "Anyone for coffee."

Matty picked up a paper and the thought struck her that all the stories were written on one side of paper only. Perhaps it was second hand paper after all her father was a solicitor and there may have been writing of some sort on the other side. "John, do you think that we might be able to sort any of the papers from the pile of ash in the corner, it might give us some clues."

"I think that is a forlorn hope but maybe having been that type of paper in this type of atmosphere has shortened its viability.".

"Perhaps there will be more clues in these," said Matty as she handed round more papers and coffee.

Issie's story was about one winter's evening when snow was frozen, Megan had visited the house by the stream and seen His Lordship having it away with Widow Hampton in the glow and warmth of the kitchen range. he dropped a monogrammed cufflink in the snow as he left in quite a hurry, it is in the wall.

"We will have to examine the walls to find this hiding place of hers," mused Chris.

"How about this then." Issie was visibly shocked. "Listen, this is how it reads.

*The days are longer now and I have to be careful that no one sees me, in the late sun I wear the cape mother made for me and can hide in the bushes. on one such night a woman in a bright blue dress with gold edges and a golden bonnet with blue edges was walking past me along the path to the smithy copse. She met a man, they kissed then swam naked in the big pool. I stole her silk knickers from the bank. in a flash another man appeared through the trees it was john enshaww pointing a gun at them ordered them out of the water and then told Iis his daughter to pick up her things and go he shouted at the man half in the water that his daughter was only sixteen pointed the gun and shot him and shot again. i screamed and ran he chased me for a while then passed close by me i waited and then had to go past the body to get home i took his jacket and money pouch and put them in the wall with the knickers.*

Every story seems tainted with blood of some kind," said John.

"We will have to look up church records and see what names turn up," said Matty, ever the sensible one.

"Wait, this one is different," said Isobel.

*Tonight i met a man who was laying traps for rabbits and hares, i watched as he put down many traps he told me he had been watching me for some time and knew i was following he told me he had some new jack russell puppies in his shed in the wood which was warm and would i like to see them they reminded me of my own baby thomas william i had named him from a grave next the church. I began crying and he put his arms around me. His name was mike and he had been living in the woods for a long time. I told him my name but not where i lived.*

*I went home and cried some more but I knew where he lived. Many nights of rain passed and after the rain stopped I went to his house again. I watched as four men chased him from the hut and shot him then set fire to it. It scorched the three sweet chestnuts in the clearing. In the light of the fire I could see Josh and three estate workers all tossing the pups into the air and onto the fire. mike lay on the ground and I covered him with my cape later i went back, he was dead i buried him with leaves stones and soil to stop the foxes from digging him up and i marked the tree nearest with an m on the south side.*

"Anyone reading these would not sleep safe in their beds around here. I wonder how many years these stories span?"
"There must be a reason for them to see daylight now."

"Look, it's two o'clock, time for us to leave it for tonight," said Chris quite firmly

In the morning Chris thought he could hear someone moving downstairs, it was only half past five, carefully picking up the bedroom door stop he crept downstairs. There in the front room was Isobel sitting at the dimly lit typewriter with her arms outstretched wearing nothing but goose pimples.

"This is not the first time you have seen me like this?"

"Err no, but what are you doing?"

"I could not sleep and thought I might encourage Megan to write more but taking off the clothes has not helped at all."

"I think you should put them back on now," worried in case Matty might wake and…

Over a cup of welcome tea Issie asked Chris about the 'other time.'

"I am not sure who would be embarrassed more you or me,"

"I will be the judge of that," she said firmly.

"It was at the cottage the day you fainted, well a few minutes before you were stood with not a stitch on," He Blushed" except a flimsy shawl that fell off as you feel and believe it or not your ordinary clothes appeared in the same instant."

"When I was Her, was my body like me or her?"

"I'm not sure I understand that," said Chris.

"Well did I look like this and her dressing gown fell off her shoulders?"

"Err yes," said Chris trying to look away.

"I wonder…"

"Wonder what?"

"If you are telling the truth now or when you were talking earlier, remember you said I had a horrendous birthmark on my face and body."

"You are right, I remember and, in the dream, as well."

"You have been dreaming about us as well? Does Matty know about this?

"Look, we are talking about Megan Frimble, not us."

"But maybe she is trying to connect to our waves?"

"What waves?"

"Kiss me."

"Isobel, this is not funny."

"Mike," she said, looking him full in the face and eyes met, and she kissed him full on the lips.

All was woodland around them with wood cut from the trees and materials to create a wooden hut. 'Megan' was humming collecting material to make a bed with while 'Mike was constructing a roof. Megan went to the streamside to collect new moss for two pillows and placed her white shawl over them.

They lay side by side his hands fell across her body, this was not the nubile woman of earlier it was a shrivelled walnut and sticky he had climbed out of his rough clothes and he too was an old sticky wrinkly. Their bodies were glued and would not fall away, this was for eternity.

Chris awoke in a real cold sweat with Matty at his side, he went to the bathroom and met Issie.

Going back to her room. "Good night's sleep." She winked.

"Err, yes I think so."

All the next day Chris seemed distant and ill at ease but that evening they continued to read scripts with tales of poaching pheasants or tickling trout from the stream, once the gamekeeper Josh had been wounded badly after a fall. And Megan had broken curfew by writing a note telling where to find him and pushing it under Widow Hampton's door. Running away, but watched the search party go look for him.

There were one or two mildly amusing stories of infidelities around the village like Vicar being seen outside Widow Hampton's back door, wearing only his dog collar while His lordship was at the front door. His lordship almost heard her laugh watching the Vicar stealing her dress from the washing line to cover his modesty while crouching at the back door.

There was a time when she saw the Smithy's lad with Lord Pressguard's daughter Poppy enjoying the stream and its eddies at the whirlpool generally having fun in and out of the water. What they had not noticed was the two horses they had ridden there on complete with clothes folded into the saddlebags had also become a little friendly and the sight of the Smithy's lad running after them was something to stir the mind.

There was a lighter side to her life when she had nursed animals and birds back to normality and the times she had set traps off in the woods or even managed to save the animals from certain death by releasing the snares and traps.

There was a much softer side to her stories when she wrote of Mike and how she wanted to hold him in her arms for eternity; he was the only man who had touched her heart. She had told in one story how she had been trapped by snow in the well tower and had hoped that if she had died there, she would be able to find him again. And be entwined in eternity.

The one story that hit home was of her thinking she was cursed for ever and her wrists were bleeding ending with her saying goodbye world.

"Could it have been the last she wrote," Matty almost whispered. "No, it is not, listen:

*I awoke yesterday morning and heard the robin singing. my arms hurt terribly. I called out but no one heard me, not even my mother. I crawled out to see my two brothers shouting about mother and the vicar and the keeper. A doctor arrived and left with them still arguing, I went into my mother's room and knelt at the bed to say the only prayer I knew. John Henry and Hubert James were still shouting and when they saw me, they saw me as a ghost with the curse on my shoulders and ran off. the next day they buried mother in the grave with father. MY two brothers were still arguing even after and they went off to Ambleside Hoe where I watched as each other pointed their guns and both guns exploded and both were dead. The smithy had heard the shots and came up to the Hoe to investigate and their bodies were taken back to the house. I said a prayer for them both.*

"The stories are beyond belief." John was shaking his head.

Absolutely incredible no one could have made that up," said Matty.

"Look," said Isobel, "Perhaps this is her last:

*My eyes are heavy today. My legs are trembling. My food is all gone and no water. I cannot walk. I must keep all my strength to find my dear Mike and stay with him.*

There is no more on this page, she must have stopped and died where we found her all alone in her prison." A tear rolled down Isobel's cheek. John went to comfort her.

"We have to do what she could not and reunite her with Mike."

"It's a bit far-fetched don't you think?" asked Chris.

"What do you think, Matty," pleaded an earnest Isobel.

"I really think we have to all stop for a moment or two and reflect on what has happened. We are dabbling in something that was not our intention to do. Perhaps we should get some professional advice from a vicar or perhaps a medium," said Matty.

"That's our Matty stolid as ever," said Chris.

Matty glared at him a little offended and went on, "The only thing is we have no corroborative evidence of anything, for all we know this is one big dream," Chris coloured up.

"We can't be sure that any odd bod that comes to the house can do any more than we can."

"That's it then we have to go as a team to the cottage and stay as a team to find something that links this all together." To his surprise they all agreed and as Chris and John had important business with the council it was decided that Saturday would be the day.

Next morning Matty rang Isobel and asked if she was up for a bit of detective work Issie agreed that they should not go to the cottage but that did not stop them going to the local church and perhaps driving around the estate to establish any corroboration evidence. "Tally ho," said Issie, "I'll pick you up in half an hour."

They found the Vicar at Frewald who had recently been ordained and was actually into looking at the church records himself; this was his first parish. "It must be our age," muttered Isobel. "He looks about fifteen."

However, the young vicar was proud that the parish records had never been lost in a fire or flood and were pretty intact since sixteen forty. Ten large bound volumes and mostly entered in copperplate writing which in itself was pretty and illuminated in a monastic way.

"You are right to be proud of these Vicar"

"Apparently Lord Pressguard was persuaded to buy this safe like cabinet to hold them safe in the fiercest fire or the deepest flood ". It resembles oakwood carved but is in fact cast metal and fully fireproofed.

They were also chronological so it was not difficult to find the late nineteenth century and the early twentieth..

"There was to be an unveiling of a plaque to honour the donation but he died before it was made according to letters and because there were no heirs that could be found it was held in abeyance until I found a record of payment made to the church at that time which was probably used for some other purpose. But the P.C.C. have kindly agreed that a new one should be made and it is to be unveiled next month. Now if you ladies will excuse me, I must prepare for Sunday, I shall be in the vestry over there and I am sure I can trust you with the books for a while."

"Thank you, Vicar."

"Oh, by the way no one is ever allowed to photograph them."

The girls spent little time scouring pages to find any references and found entries for *Derek Frimble Died June 12* and of *Mary Jane Frimble* a month later and here as an aside the burial of John Henry and *Hubert James* in unconsecrated ground for paupers and those who take their own lives, so one assumes it was supposed to be a suicide pact of some sort.

Isobel found an entry for an *Albert Edgson Aged 19* who drowned after a shooting accident in 1912 "remember the young man floating in the river."

"Yes, you are right, let's delve a little more."

"Oh, look at this christened 14th may 1913 Thomas Willian Young."

"Sorry to interrupt ladies but I have parish business to attend to and I can't leave the books out."

"Perhaps we could come back another day," inquired Isobel.

Perhaps even on Sunday morning" said the quick-thinking vicar.

"Well, we are about to become your parishioners at Melfort so maybe we will become regulars."

"It was my vain attempt at humour I am afraid," said the vicar. "If you let me know when and where I can acquaint you with some of the regulars of the village."

"Actually, Vicar we are getting acquainted with some of the villagers already but that is for another day, thank you for letting us see the books."

"Please do. It is nice to have some interest in church matters and despite what I said I am here most mornings between ten and twelve." he shook their hands and scooted off.

"Wait a minute," said Matty. "The gravestone, remember it was by the church door."

They searched but found nothing.

"You looking for something," the voice came from nowhere.

"Over here and down."

It was the gravedigger just emerging from a freshly dug hole.

"Didn't mean to frighten you, Peter Edgson please excuse me for not shaking hands.

Only the clay is really sticky hereabouts.

"No, that's alright Mr Edgson, we were looking for a gravestone near the church door."

"They was all moved a couple of year ago all stood against the back wall."

"I don't suppose you remember Thomas William among them."

"Of course, the Thomas William with no surname, come see, there is a grey headstone with no surname carved in it. It was to be levied that the old squire had that made for his cat and the stone mason that carved it did not finish it on the account of dying but the staff put it up anyway.

"Thank you for your trouble, Mr Edgson."

"No trouble, it is nice to talk to someone alive in this neck of the woods." He laughed. As he prepared the grave, ready for the incoming vicar and funeral party.

"Alright, where have you two been?" said Chris sitting on the sofa with a beer in hand and John at his side also with a beer.

"Just couldn't wait, eh," said John.

"Then where...," asked John, Chris's meeting was cancelled and as I was not needed either we thought we would pick you up and go foraging.

"We've been to see the vicar of our future parish church," said Matty.

"I didn't know there was a church at Melfort," queried John.

"There isn't clever clogs, it's at Frewald," mused Issie.

"Never mind," said Chris. "Let's have a Chinese takeaway and you can tell us all about the crusty old vicar. And his churchyard."

"It's our shout," said Issie, "and if John drops me off on the way there by the time, he comes back I can have packed a few things for tonight and tomorrow I can't see us not stopping over tonight if you don't mind Matty."

"Not at all, I know that cheap plonk from France last year is pretty potent." She laughed.

An hour later they were tucking into the meal with some gusto.

"You know we are tending to forget that there is a serious side to all this adventure and we still have a house to build and renovate."

"You are so right Chris, but we have to deal with this uneasy ghost that is holding us back."

"Are we the right people to ease the spirit into wherever she needs to be.

"We have been chosen," said Issie.

"Okay, I will go along with the mumbo jumbo bit but at the end of the day it is a huge financial, not sentimental, investment!"

"Well folks, a seven o'clock start in the morning so we had better get some shut-eye. Matty, why don't you and I make some sandwiches for tomorrow while these two use the facilities."

"Good idea, boss," she said, leading him to the kitchen.

"John, would you really advise pulling the plug on this house, would you?" asked Issie.

"No, not really but I just feel I am on the edge of this and I want to get more involved."

"Good," she said as she cuddled him closer.

She drifted off into dreamland close in his arms and he lay there thinking what it must have been like then, for Megan to have only the nighttime as company. He wondered how many people had and indeed are now suffering from these strange almost mystical birthmarks. How many in the past did not make it past childbirth or were so hideous that they were bricked into rooms never to be seen. At least Megan had the night as freedom and her mother for some time to care and protect her. She would have been like a nocturnal fox stirring on the nights when clear and even sniffing the air for danger, allowing her eyes to get used to the limited light and only then stepping out into the night, his thoughts carried him with her, in an aura of mystery travelling with great speed and agility through the well-trodden pathways in the undergrowth. With such stealth that not even a twig cracked. Instinctively, she waded into the fast-running stream shedding her white shawl on the bank to bathe in the cool water, coloured by the moonlight above. The water glistened on her body like diamonds brilliant and dazzling as it dripped back into nature's vault. She walked from the water and replaced her shawl covering the rags and tatters under it. Clasping her hands on his she led him on to the woodland clearing, there she pointed to the ground and then to the big house in the distance, with not a word. Putting her finger to her lips she motioned out to the meadow where two fox cubs were playing, practising their skills for future survival. A hand gripped his shoulder directing his head to the other side of the wood, an arm raised a rifle glinting in the moonlight, the shot rang out. One of the cubs ran for cover in the trees, the other lay still on the grassy slope. Megan had quiet tears running down her face and John tried to put his arms around her to comfort her. Only moments passed as the cub that ran for cover crept out to its playmate but only found a useless lump that was just sniffable. The man with the rifle also crept into the open obviously to get a clear shot. John Lunged forward and shouted, there was a long yellowish flash and he fell to the ground in agony his hand went to his chest and could feel the warm blood oozing between his fingers. Megan was at his side frantically trying to cover the body, HIS BODY, with soil stones and leaves. he could see the blood from her burning hands as she toiled endlessly, soil and stones covered his legs and it was creeping up to his crossed arms and bloody chest. He screamed and flung his arms up *I AM NOT DEAD.*

He sat up in bed and threw the covers off. "It's alright, John dear, just a dream." She cradled him while he was frantically checking his body for blood. There was nothing, not even a scratch. He thanked God it had not been real.

"What time is it, Issie?"

"Eleven thirty."

"At night…" He realised the room was filled with moonlight from the large full moon outside.

"I was dreaming."

"I gathered that, dear."

"I can't remember what about."

"Never mind for now, just get some sleep."

"I can't sleep with the moonlight shining through the curtains."

"I'll close them, it will keep the wee ghoulies and ghosties out." She smiled.

"Don't mock me." As he said that, he could see the moonlight just catching the body curves and felt a tinge of disappointment, but Issie was determined to render him back to sleep and slipped off the nightdress.

At seven thirty, suitably fuelled with a full English and enough sandwiches to feed an army, they set off for the house. They arrived as the last of the morning mist was clearing, boding a clear dry day to follow, just perfect for exploration. "What first, boss?"

"All got torches and brushes for cobwebs. Let's see if we can find the wall with the cache in."

Chris pointed out that some of the walls might be unstable so not too much pushing. "We'll start at the tunnel end and work our way round. Issie and John, if you don't mind, go that way and Matty and I will go this way."

After an hour of feeling along the tunnel, they were all in the room and carefully checked all the crevices. Matty held the torch and all of a sudden, she felt a cold chill from a window-type opening, just a small one, but there was something odd about the way the strata of the rock lay and it was slightly ill fitting. At one side of the stone was a small slit that Chris tried to pull at but it would not shift. "We are going to need some help."

"You rang, sir." It was John with his torch shining upwards.

"You…" It was a few moments while Chris put his scramble brain into gear but noticed just above John's head was a bent piece of steel. Chris's hand went right past John's ear making him think that perhaps he had stretched the friendship a little too far but the hand grabbed the metal key above his head.

Chris put the 'key' into the slit and turned it ninety degrees, then both pulled and the stone moved groaning until the hinges broke and John just managed to avoid the falling stone.

"Look," said Matty, her torch shone on a pile of old clothes and a box.

Taking everything out carefully they took it all to the outdoor light, the clothes had disintegrated so badly like the paper they were not really identifiable but there was the box.

John expected it to be stuck but there was no resistance and the lid opened freely.

Issie gasped. Inside, in absolute perfect condition, were two long strings of pearls. A red glass brooch that was cut to shine at every angle, a necklace of what looked like marcasite, some green glass beads, drop earrings and a pair of cufflinks.

As Matty pulled them out one by one, she found a piece of card and underneath there were three watches, a hip flask with a silvered monogram not easily distinguished in this light, a leather pouch with two Hal sovereigns, four pennies and a silver threepence and a broken riding crop which Issie dropped almost as quickly as she had picked it up..

"I don't know about you but this is a bit beyond belief."

Lunch was next and ignoring the sandwiches they brushed the cobwebs off and went to the pub.

Obviously, the topic of conversation was all about what to do next.

As they came out of the pub, Chris noticed a jeweller's shop, a quiet unassuming little shop, and Chris suggested they take a couple of the items there to evaluate them after all they were not experts.

Inside the pokey little shop which was a bit like an Aladdin's cave, everything glistened and shone. A smart young man in a town suit asked if he could help.

"We were wondering if there was someone here who could help us to identify some jewellery that we have found in a sort of safe in a wall of a property we have recently bought."

Chris put one of the necklaces and the glass brooch and the green glass necklace on the counter.

"For what purpose do you require the valuation?"

"I'm sorry, I don't understand "

"Is it for insurance purposes or for sale valuation or just curiosity."

"All three I suppose but perhaps we might have to declare them as treasure troves."

"You say they were in a safe of sorts in a house, that means treasure trove rules do not apply and the items would belong to the owner of the house. Now this is a quality string of pearls strung around the 1890s, he put it to one side. This is a ruby brooch set in 22ct gold circa 1850 and…" he said picking up the necklace, "is something I think my father might like to see again."

He called his father. "I think I am right." He looked at his father. The oldish man pushed his glasses up over his forehead.

"Where did you get this from?"

"As I told your son, we found these in a sort of safe in a cottage nearby."

"Forgive my curiosity, but this fine piece of jewellery was made by my grandfather from the finest rubies brought back from India. My father was asked to make a copy of this in paste some sixty years ago when the late lord Pressguard had apparently lost the original. So, you see that after four generations of knowledge of its existence made me curious."

"Wow!"

"My son here recognised the maker's marks which can be seen under a high-powered lens just here.

"Would you be able to put a value on these," asked John.

"Without provenance it is difficult but I would probably guess at five to six thousand…for the pearls, the ruby is about two thousand and the necklace around one hundred and fifty thousand pounds."

Matty went weak at the knees and sat down.

"Bit of a shock," said the old man, this happens all the time with older jewels.

Issie asked if they could keep them in the shop's secure room for a while.

"Certainly, and we will clean them for free, then we will see their real beauty."

The young man gave them their receipts and it was back to base for the four.

"I think we have to convene a proper board meeting between the four of us," said Chris.

"I would hate to think where this could lead us and I would want us to remain friends whatever."

At that meeting, they decided the police had to be involved to make everything legal and they would have all the items appraised. They decided that monies from sales of those items would be used to improve the house or whatever it needed. So, it was the police first. They said that as it had been found on the property that they had legitimately bought then the contents, provided they had not been reported as stolen, were the property of the owner.

There were no reports of any of the items being stolen so that ended that little part of the saga.

They had all the items itemised and individually valued at a total of six hundred and fifty thousand pounds less some commission on sales.

That was a huge amount to put into the building fund and probably a holiday.

Another meeting ensued to decide what to do and when.

They drew up and kept to an agenda.

1.  Did they still want to keep and continue to renovate the property or did they want to sell it off and effectively run. Vote.. all in favour of staying.
2.  Did they want to keep any of the jewellery? Vote.. all in favour sell it.
3.  We need to investigate the happenings and possibly involve the new vicar. Vote … all in favour.
4.  There are a lot of inexplicable things so are we prepared to continue and Issie, for whatever reasons you seem more heavily involved than most… Vote…all in favour.
5.  "I feel," said Chris, "that if we are to be happy having the neighbours, we have that we should keep the stories under our own hats for now as we don't want to alienate the neighbours we will have for years and years"…Vote…all say aye.

6.  I feel, said Issie, that we should ask permission from the estate owner to have a wander to establish the physical possibilities of the stories and it might just put some to bed as it were. All agreed Chris would get in touch with the buyer's agent to get permission.


Chris did get permission and the lady and gentleman, Australian, would not be taking up residence for two months so feel free and they would love to meet them when they are in residence.

The next morning, they stood at the second well head and tried to decide which way Megan would have travelled at night. "I would have said easterly to keep the moon shining in front of her"

"Makes sense," said Chris. "We have all day, let's go east." Looks at the compass, he said, "That way."

"She would not have gone directly, would she, people would have spotted her in the middle of a field in moonlight. She would have taken the hedgerow route with the hedge as a backdrop."

In the next field, they perceived that the big field would have been smaller fields back then and sure enough on the 1920 ordinance survey map, it was indeed three fields.

As they reached the corner of the wood, as it would have been, John felt a cold chill and stiffened.

"I've been here before," said John. "Call it what you like, deja vous, I have definitely been on this spot before."

"Is this another of your poor-quality jokes?" Issie was not amused. "Cos if it is, it's in bloody awful taste."

John was white as a sheet and sweating profusely. "John, are you okay?" She was worried now.

"Norman Aylesthorpe is buried here," said John.

"Where?" said Chris just holding Issie back.

John spun on the spot and pointed to the mound of earth close to the hedge.

At that moment a pheasant clattered from the undergrowth and startled John. His colour had returned. "Are we ready to go on."

"John," inquired Issie, "what happened here a few minutes ago."

"We crossed the field and a pheasant flew out of the undergrowth."

"Nothing else."

"No, why, what happened?"

"Does the name Norman Aylesthorpe mean anything to you?" asked Matty.

"No, I don't think so. What is this all about?"

They told him what just happened. "In my dream you remember Issie, I was shot and was being buried near a wood."

"X marks the spot," said Chris..

They walked over to the mound but found no marks of disturbance but it might have been a long time there without anyone noticing. But John knew this was the spot.

"Do we tell the police."

"Tell them what? No policeman is going to believe this crazy story…We dig." Holding his spade in hand, Chris turned over the turf and there was nothing, then the very next second, Matty told him to stop. "There is a bone there."

Explaining to a police inspector that they had just uncovered a second body in the middle of nowhere after the bones found in the house was stretching his imagination a little far. He had the rest of this body exhumed and asked them who it might be. "We think a Norman Aylesthorpe."

She had no evidence for any of the happenings and the bones were taken away.

With no way of identifying the body other than the word of the four and any tests they could do, they had to inter the body in a Christian grave.

"If you find any more bodies just let me know," he said.

The four were quite shaken by the ease at which they had found the body; they had exhausted their need for adventure that day. The next day, Chris did have to work and John had to take Issie to visit a very poorly and elderly aunt in hospital. So that left Matty on her own all day. She quickly dashed around the house cleaning and shoving a load in the washer, then she was out of there. At Frewald church, she found the newly dug very small grave which she assumed were the interred bones. She left a little posy of flowers in a jam jar on the grave and went on to Melfort. Sure enough she found Young Josh on the steps. He had not met Matty before and he screwed his eyes up to try and establish who she was. She asked him about Norman Aylesford.

"You related?"

"My Grandfather's brother," she lied. "We believe he was a Gamekeeper hereabouts back in 1910."

"There was a Norman Aylesford around at that time but he was one for the ladies and it was believed that he had buggered off with some young woman, eloped to Scotland on account he was seventeen without so much as a by your leave."

"Do you happen to know who the young lady was?"

"None of my business," and with that he got up and went.

Matty was still curious and went back to the church hoping to catch the new vicar.

She found him polishing the candlesticks from the altar.

"Hello again."

"You remember me, I hope I am not intruding."

"No, not at all, please sit down."

"Well, the thing is, my husband and I, also two friends are trying to help someone settle affairs in the family and allow them to rest in peace."

"Sounds like an intriguing pottage, would it have to do with the record search the other day."

"Well yes, look vicar, if I tell you all about this will you promise not to tell a soul."

"Are you telling me as a Vicar or a confidant?"

"Both really."

"Then I am to tell you that should there be a reason to tell the police, I am bound by law to divulge, or if it brings the church into disrepute."

"I am all agog in anticipation."

Matty decided there was no reason to hold back and told him the bare bones of the story and how they were attempting to put Megan to rest.

"My…that is a fine story but how can I help?"

"You already have, vicar, just by listening. You see although none of us are deeply religious, we may need some sort of spiritual guidance for Megan. Don't ask me how or why but I think there is more to know about Megan and at some stage her bones will have to be put to rest.

"I don't see any problem with the latter, we know her given name and she is of this parish, her death is not by her own hand and therefore she could be buried near to her kin. There would be a plot charge of course but not a lot."

"Thank you, Vicar."

"Please, if you need me, then give me a call, my name is Roger by the way, Roger Davis. Here is my number." "Thank you Roger, oh I almost forgot, what happened to the old vicar here."

"Put out to grass at the vicar's retirement home in Bournemouth. Unfortunately, he had a serious stroke a couple of months ago, watching at the last day of the auction sale and subsequently cannot speak or hear anything."

"Oh, how sad."

When Chris came home, he looked forlorn so Matty's exploits would have to wait. "What is wrong, dear?"

He handed her the letter that council employees dread most of the time. 'Due to administration restructuring and departmental changes it is necessary to ask for persons who are eligible for a redundancy scheme to consider voluntary early retirement.'

"Does this mean people specifically, inquired Matty.

The letter doesn't but the visit from the council chairman is more personal he mentioned very subtly that the government severance scheme was pay plus enhancement of pension pots and if certain 'older' members of staff took early retirement from mainstream employment there could be room for the younger element at a lower rate and the chance of possible consultancy work on a more ad hoc basis.

"How do you feel about it."

"On the one hand it is a kick in the teeth but on the other it is an opportunity to rid myself of the whinging joe public for the next ten years."

"When do you have to decide?"

"By the end of next week there is to be a meeting on Friday to discuss next steps. Let's invite John and Issie over for a drink."

"I already did, John has had a similar letter and 'chat'

They sat around the table and considered their options.

It's cards on the table time.

Agenda …… Assets.

Outgoings.

Income

Possibilities.

"Who is going to start?"

"I will," said John.

Assets One house approx. 20000 all furniture paid for savings about 2000 now after paying half of the house. There could be a hefty pay out from the council but not guaranteed.

Van belongs to the council but I may have the chance to purchase it.

Issie added there was his endowment insurance and of course a regular pension.

"Right," said Chris.

House 20000 plus no outstanding debts savings now improved since half of this house is sold, has a car also has endowment insurance and of course a pension to come.

"You know," said Matty, "it is clear what we should do. Pool resources. We are going to live in the same albeit different parts of a house, why not sell one of our houses now and move in together. We rub along quite nicely and we can spend more time organising the renovations that other people are doing for us. We could use the money from the sale to buy materials and we will save on utility bills just to pay half."

"How do you feel about sharing a kitchen, Issie?"

"No problem, one of you men can do the washing up one week and the other the next in rotation."

Chris immediately suggested to John "A dishwasher." They laughed.

"We will have to have some sort of legal agreement for the sake of children but let's drink to our future venture together."

"And of course," said Matty, "we have our surprise find to share. Many thanks to Megan."

Matty had almost forgotten her news of the day and recounted her meeting with the vicar.

"That's great, that means another villain of the peace is out of the fray and if we can put Megan to a peaceful end then things will improve."

"We still have Mike to put to rest, he is out there somewhere."

No time like the present said Chris in all bravado if a little tipsy. "If Megan could troll those woods in the dark I am sure we can with torches. and the moonlight."

Matty thought it was mad but she had had the least to drink and was safest to drive.

Armed with torches, compass and the O.S. Map, they went down the Melfort Road. Matty had the strange desire to stop and did so. When almost at a standstill, a small whirlwind picked up a dust cloud in front of them and threw it across the field. One would have been forgiven for thinking that Martians had arrived.

"Over there… are they not sweet chestnut trees with those long crinkly leaves."

"You could be right Matty, and there are not many of them in these woods. Let's go and investigate."

All prepared with walking boots they set off across the field to the little copse and sure enough there were three rather large sweet chestnut trees.

Chris was wondering if chestnut trees lasted that long, the mark that was made would have been sufficient to be still there. Matty found the mark all crusted and gnarled but quite clear on the south side of the tree.

"Hey, look at this, the compass pointer won't stop spinning."

Isobel walked to his side and as she stood there, a chill ran up and down her spine.

"He's here," she said.

"Issie!" He looked at her in disbelief.

"He's here, I'll tell you."

"Chris!" pleaded Matty. Issie has been right all along, why should we doubt her now."

"Okay, mark the spot with some stones and we can come back in daylight."

Matty turned to look for some stones and came face to face with two barrels of a shotgun.

"Now, would you mind telling me what four grown up adults are doing in my woods at this time of night?"

He had seen them get out of the car and thought they might be badger hunters or worse some sort of witches' sect out in his woods. They certainly were not poachers making all that racket.

"Excuse me." Chris was being bold. "There is no need for any gun."

"I'll be the judge of that, thank you, now I think some sort of explanation is in order."

"We are on a night treasure hunt and our instructions were to find the three trees by turning right after Brewald."

"Then you are barking up the wrong tree as they say," said the gamekeeper, breaking and lowering his gun. "You must have made the wrong turning in Melfort and the three trees is the three oaks pub on the Cretham Road."

"You must think we're real idiots but look, the compass is spinning like crazy."

"Strange things do happen round here in the middle of the night when the moon is full." He moved away laughing his head off.

"That'll earn him a pint or two."

"Now let's get out of here we can come back tomorrow."

"You realise that the inspector is never going to believe that we have found yet another body in the woods."

"Then we won't tell him. What harm can it do to bury these bones if they are there with Megan, assuming we can have them released from the laboratory."

"Three things," said John. "One; we will be obstructing the police in their duty, two; we will be perverting the course of justice and three we will be aiding and abetting a criminal."

"Oh, shut up you old fuddy duddy, where is your sense of adventure?" said Issie. A brandy nightcap soon had John off to sleep.

The heavy rain the next morning made the two men believe that it would hinder any significant progress in their digging, but they had not counted on the fact that Issie and Matty had already been gone an hour and were gently but firmly picking all the bones from the little mound of stones and earth. "What have we started, Matty?"

Matty was not listening; she was making sure they had all the bones including the skull all in a neat plastic bag.

Matty was completely entranced and took the plastic bag to the boot of the car. Isobel drove back to the house and Matty placed the bag on the table in the room where they had found Megan. They then drove home to find a police car outside.

"Mrs Jenkins and Mrs Wardhay, are your husbands about?"

"No, it looks like they have gone for a walk. Can we help?"

"In the circumstances, probably you can. In regards to the skeletal remains." They both went bright pink or thought so. "You will remember that the remains that were found appeared to have no reason for anything other than a natural death and therefore our forensic team have no further use of the skeletal remains. Do you happen to know if there are any living relatives of the deceased because quite frankly these are a source of embarrassment to us. And if we don't find anyone to take care of the skeletal remains, we will have to destroy them."

"Inspector, would it be possible for us to arrange for a committal for the skeleton."

"I was hoping you might say that as you are the nearest thing to a relative, you will have to arrange a vicar and an undertaker but they will act discreetly.

"Thank you for being so understanding. Good day ladies."

"Bye Inspector. Oh damn, it is gone twelve and the vicar will be gone from the church. Oh wait, I have his number somewhere. Roger Davis Melfort 746.

Mr Davis, Roger, do you remember me, Mathilda Jenkins? We spoke the other day about Megan Frimble. You remember me, good. Could my friend and I come over and discuss a service with you. Oh good, this afternoon would be great. Say three, thank you, see you then."

Just time for some lunch.

When John and Chris arrived home together that evening, they were not happy. Chris had been informed that he had a choice of early retirement or enforced redundancy. As he and Matty had discussed it, he signed for early retirement what he had not expected was the American style of progression and immediacy ending with his desk being cleared into a box and the car keys taken from him, an ignominious handshake from the mayor and on your bike. Fortunately, John's boss was in Edinburgh and wants to see him in the morning John gave me a lift home in his van which he will no doubt lose tomorrow as well.

"We called at Freddy's garage thinking he might not have heard anything but the council are cutting back on six cars that he is purchasing from them that Percival wastes no time."

"We have looked at a four-wheel drive Land Rover so we can tow a trailer. It's two grand but it's what we will need for taking stuff to the cottage. We will buy it together and I will insure it for any driver. "We need you to take us there to collect it if you would please."

"Of course. What a rotten day for you."

Matty thought this was not the time to tell that they had arranged for Roger to perform a service for Megan and that they had Mike's bones at the house in a plastic bag ready to put in the coffin with Megan's old bones. The undertaker was to take the coffin to the church for a nine o'clock service at the graveside. Matty and Issie would go to the church, apparently the lid would not be screwed down as any stillborn child could be discreetly disposed of in the coffin. They would go there early in the morning and add Mike's bones. Job done. They would talk to John and Chris later when they had calmed down. And had a bag of chips.

John and Issie stayed over but hardly anyone slept thinking about what the day would bring, John was about to be kicked out of a job, Chris was to sign on at the job centre, Matty and Issie had their duty to perform in total secrecy of the two lads. John wanted a really early start to go through papers at work before they were rifled so both men went, leaving Matty and Issie about an hour to get the bones to the church. When they got to the church, Roger was already there dusting and polishing.

"My, you are early!"

"Cold in here," said Matty.

"Hmm takes a while for the heating to get going, perhaps a cup of Tea in the vicarage might warm you."

"Yes, please," said Matty.

"I will go and put the kettle on then, and will be back in a minute or two."

Matty took the lid off the coffin to see just a black body bag with a zip. Issie went to the car and came back with the other bag. They quickly tipped the bag inside the zip and had the lid on just as Roger came back with the tea on a tray.

"Would you like to pour while I screw the lid on, it is my duty to do so and the undertakers will be here soon."

The interment was very brief but done in solemness with just the vicar, the girls and the gravedigger, even the undertakers had gone. Matty gave the gravedigger a tip and they left him filling the hole with such speed.

Everything seemed to be happening at once, John was beaten to work by his young spotty replacement already installed at his desk and boxes of stuff were by the door, OUTSIDE.

There was a note asking him to leave keys and passes at the reception. Furious at the way all FOURTEEN of them were booted out they went to the Fox and Grapes for a goodbye libation and communal moan. But as it turned out, the Council buggers had done them a favour, no false goodbyes and good luck, no useless clocks and freedom in front of them.

Matty and Issie had decided to not even mention the funeral, so they went to the office and paid for the 'Cheapest coffin' as was promoted by the director. "Well, we did it, they are reunited." They embraced.

Back at home there was a message that someone wanted to view John and Issie's house so it would be all hands-on deck to clean. The people came and went. They went back to Chris and Matty's house for lunch.

Sitting at the dinner table all of a sudden there was a gust of wind and a piece of paper blew up and floated to the floor. It had two words, "Thank You.

"Look," said Chris as the letters disappeared, and the letters on all the papers disappeared, with the papers turning to dust, which a cold chill swept them through the open door.

"Matty, Issie, what have you done?" said Chris.

Matty and Issie had to 'come clean' and told them of their exploits.

"Look at the typewriter," said John and there it sat rusty and unclean with a white cloth over it.

"Perhaps all this is now over with Megan Frimble put to rest."

A sound night's sleep had them all raring to go to the cottage to begin in all seriousness the planning for renovation, but just as they were leaving the Estate Agent rang to say the house was sold and the new people would like to move as soon as paperwork could be completed.

He put the phone down and it rang again.

"They have changed their minds," said Chris, "but it was the jeweller inviting them to go to the shop to see the cleaned items."

Arriving at the little jeweller's shop, they were met by both father and son, shown to the private viewing room. This was not for the hustle and bustle of the shop floor.

The jewels they had left were on view in proper display boxes and looked stunning. The pearls took on the sheen of the cream-coloured interior of the box. The Brooch was on a rouge base and looked on fire as the light shone through and reflected as though it was a fire base. The earrings sparkled with an iridescence. The father then, as if by magic, produced a long box dark black and when opened the piece de resistance laid elegantly in a cream lace. The light danced all over the walls of the room as it moved; it did not even look red.

"May I put it on?" said Matty.

"That is what my father made it for, to be worn on the neck of a beautiful and elegant lady please wear and enjoy."

She stood as he gently put the necklace around her neck and motioned her to the mirror.

"Not bad for a few bits of glass," chuckled Chris.

"It's gorgeous Issie. You try it on."

Issie felt a cold chill and declined, the old man gently undid the clasp and replaced it into the box. "They are absolutely fantastic," said Matty.

"Fine work is always a pleasure to see and to fondle this after so many years."

"You have seen it before "

"It was indeed my pleasure to have been here in the shop when his Lordship came in to purchase it. His Lordship paid for it in cash and took it away to give it to lady Margaret at the May Ball the following week."

"So, this belonged to Lady Margaret?" asked Chris.

"It was to have been but tragedy struck that week when she and her horse fell over a cliffside on the estate and she broke her neck. Nothing was ever heard of it since. My father always considered that it was a waste of time in the making if it was never to be worn. He would have been ecstatic to see you wearing it today.

"Would you care for some tea?" said the younger man.

The older man went on as the tea in the very finest of china was being served. "Would you be surprised if I told you that there has been some interest shown in these jewels, I cannot of course divulge who the client is but needless to say we and yourselves need to establish provenance and proof that they have been recorded as stolen or not. You have told my son here that you bought them as part of a house and fittings. I have established on the quiet that they have never been registered as stolen."

"So, what happens now?'' said Chris.

"They are indeed valuable and therefore you should inform the police and if no legitimate owner is found, they will indeed become your property to dispose of as you wish." The older man looked over his glasses and took a deep breath.

"Now, I think is the right time for me to make you an offer on behalf of a client…My client shall remain anonymous throughout these dealings and is prepared to make you a once only offer of two hundred and fifty thousand pounds for the necklace and the pearls. The payment will be in cash and we as the original makers will supply the client with a new bill of sale, on the sworn basis that it was never found. I shall withdraw for you to discuss the matter."

"Wow, do we sell or do we sell?" said Issie.

"Vote time. All in favour say aye, all against say no."

With silence on the latter, the vote was done and dusted…

Chris was having second thoughts when the look of you silly bugger from Matty put paid to any thoughts like that..

"A sensible decision I must say and by the way, I was instructed not to negotiate over price."

"Now, I must inform the purchaser so if you would excuse me, he motioned to the door."

"A quarter of a million quid, wow," said John.

"Megan must have meant for us to have the jewels. Otherwise, she would not have shown us the hiding place," said Issie. "It is such a pity that she never got to enjoy the rewards."

"Look," said Chris, "Let's have the remaining pearls split into two strings and the emeralds into two pendants for you two girls to share while Chris and I have a watch each. We can sell the rest or perhaps give the other watch back to Josh. All agreed."

Lunch at the Flying Fox was the order of the day…

That evening, looking for clues as to which was in fact Josh's watch, they looked again through the papers but they were all blank. Then Issie came into the room in her nightdress.

"Pinch me somebody, this is a dream."

Issie was sleeping in the chair while the other Issie was standing in front of them.

In a dark toned voice, the standing Issie spoke, "The secrets die and are buried with me. Thank you and GOODBYE…they all watched as she faded into the typewriter and the roller turned winding the white nightdress into the machine. A cold chill hit the room and Issie woke up.

"What…" she said, "did I nod off?"

"Err, yes," said John. He would tell her tomorrow perhaps. "Busy day tomorrow."

The morning brought a phone call at 8.30. It was Mr Eidelson, the jeweller, who wanted them to go to the shop at 10.00 if possible.

By ten thirty, they each had a check for 250,000 pounds and they had organised for the other jewellery to be cleaned and re-mounted etc and Mr Eidelson was to sell the ruby if he could. Also, they wanted 'love from Megan' inscribed on the back of the watches as a memento.

Having some time on their hands they decided to find out where Josh lived. The only starting place was perhaps the pub.

Chris asked the bespectacled barman if he knew of Josh, the man they were talking to the other day in the bar.

"You mean Young Josh."

"Yes. He is at the undertakers, died yesterday morning of a heart attack at 9.00 in the morning just to prove that the local folklore was wrong folks reckoned he had no heart."

"Oh, I see."

"You will be wanting his address I suppose."

"No, thanks."

"It will be boot hill for him from Tuesday onwards."

"Landlord, we have a watch that apparently belonged to Josh and there are no relatives that we know, do you think you could hang it on the beam up there."

"More bloody dusting." But he hung it up anyway.

When they got back to the house, the sun was beaming onto the yellowing trees and the house looked picturesque, peace and tranquillity oozed everywhere.

Chris turned to Matty and John to Issie. "Ain't life just grand."

"Sure is, Pardner."

That night should have been *the happy ever after* start they had hoped for but somehow Issie knew they had not seen the last of the Frimbles.

John and Issie sold their house and moved in with Chris and Matty, each taking it in turns week by week to play host to each other and Chris was not spurred on by their buyer wanting the house but not for nine months or so.

Half Moon house was starting to look like it should with lots of modernisations happening due to the extra finance from the jewellery sales. They did some of the work themselves and also employed interested builders trying to emulate the high-quality finish. They were careful not to overdo the budget and they wanted to be part of the restoration project themselves to have a proudness.

They stripped ivy off a lot of the walls and they also knew it was a case of managing the beast only gained by mastering it in the first place. Care taken in only cutting small sections off the wall helped except in one case where a block was dislodged and missed a couple of Chris's toes by inches. When Chris looked up to thank the ever-watchful God, he noticed a bottle in the wall. A glass bottle that would have held processed fruit or something, but in this case, it was sealed with a large cork bung and sealing wax with a seal impressed into it.

"Well said Chris, do we tell the girls or not?"

A label stuck on the inside to be read from the outside, it is in copperplate writing and reads:

'To whom it concerns, this jar has been placed here within this wall to demonstrate life and times of the end of the nineteenth century. Yours most truly, DEREK ARTHUR FRIMBLE.'

"The thing will be, do we tell the girls or indeed anyone of its existence or do we politely put it back as though we had never seen it."

"We will have to tell them in the end so let's take it back to the kitchen and open it carefully perhaps photograph it all and then add more items from today and reseal it with some desiccant inside to help preserve it and then replace it in the wall."

They decided not to open the papers as it might help them to disintegrate but instead carefully wrote the date it was opened and replaced plus a few personal items of the age including six lead coins fashioned by the plumber each with a punched name on his, Frank, Matty, Issie, Chris and John, and they included one for Megan. All carefully wrapped and dropped into the jar. There was also a photograph of the house with scaffolding and the group of four. This was all put into some concrete and stone mix and replaced in the wall.

The time for the house buyer to return and need their house prompted them to make a big push.

The scaffold was taken down in a day all in piles and iron grid boxes a maze of padlocks shackles and tubes, all ready for collection the day following.

"Came down quicker than it went up."

"Always does, looks different now."

They both stood back and looked at Half Moon House with a lot of satisfaction being restored back to its former health and improved with modern conveniences.

"Only the garden to do now, Boy," said Matty M mockingly.

"There's all the inner stone ring to do and some painting first."

"Just joking, it looks wonderful and well done."

One month later, just as promised they vacated the hustle and bustle of their town house and moved into the idyllic country retreat.

Chris and John reminded themselves and were also lucky that the council that had ousted them, left them pretty much to their own devices out there in the sticks, just what they had achieved, a sympathetic restoration, trying to get into the mindset of Derek Frimble and all his turmoil whilst innovating modern usage without spoiling the old-world character that had drawn their attention in the first place.

Although they were such good friends and now neighbours, it was decided that any interior changes were made by each on their own to try and give them a little privacy.

During a fine day when they were out on the make do for now patio that they were deciding what to do with the rest of the stone they had when a man turned up dressed in a work suit and tie.

Chris immediately thought this was one of the upstarts from his old office who came to put the cat among the pigeons.

"Excuse me, but is this The Half Moon House?"

"It is, who is asking."

"My name is Robert Joshua Frimble."

Chris paled, Matty sat down and Issie felt a shudder down her spine.

"I am on vacation to England and whilst here I thought I might get involved in genealogy and trace some of my ancestry."

"What leads you to here," asked John straight to the point as ever.

"My grandfather apparently."

"Thomas William?" blurted out Matty.

"How did you know?" he said, sensing that he was on prickly ground here.

"Just a guess."

"As I was saying, my grandfather Thomas William Frimble came from Melfort, was raised as a foundling by a Mr and Mrs Allsopp at Tingleton cottage. Thomas joined a travelling circus over here from America and went back with them ending up in Pittsburgh where he married my grandmother, Alicia. They had my dad whom they named Joshua after a gamekeeper to Lord somebody or other over here, and my dad married with them having twin boys, me and my brother James Henry…"

The four sat open mouthed.

Chris broke the silence and invited Robert to go into the house.

"It all looks very cosy yet modern. Lovely that it has no squared corners, everything in the states is so square and clinical, but this is quaint and so welcoming."

"Robert, thanks for the compliments but we have literally spent months in and around this house with renovations and repairs and only moved in a few days ago. We have had to do a lot of your family history digging locally, we therefore have quite a few stories. Most of which we cannot corroborate with facts. We do know that this house was owned at one time by a Derek Frimble who had two sons. We believe that Derek Frimble designed the original house and Lord Pressguard had some sort of reversion deed that brought the house back to the estate when no relatives were found. We believe that the origin of this deed was because the land was won on the turn of a card. We bought this place when the estate was totally broken up after the death of Lord Pressguard.

"Hey you guys, I get the feeling that I am here to cause some sort of upset in your arrangements, let me assure you I am not and nor will my brother. All I came to do was to establish any facts or indeed fictions, and take a few photographs. Would you mind if I brought a professional photographer over say tomorrow and take some pictures so I can show them to my wife and my brother? It is so delightful."

Chris glanced at the others and said "Of course."

When he had gone, deep discussions took place about MEGAN. They decided that this young man would have to have a little more proof than just a traveller from the states. If all the stories were related as true there may be some sort of claim on the estate especially with all the jewellery.

John was to go to the solicitors in the morning to see what could be done.

He sat in a large office-type chair at the solicitors expecting to see some crusty old bespectacled bloke but had been pleasantly surprised to have met this attractive and charming lady on the other side of the desk. She introduced herself as the conveyancing expert Miss Karen Young, and how could she help.

John explained how the situation had come about and expressed their fears about this young American man coming on the scene at this stage with perhaps thoughts of 'taking back some inheritance.'

"I can assure you that as we have all the documentation relating to the sale that ownership and title were established. So, in the first instance if there was any kind of claim it would be on the Pressguard estate and not you." She went on. "Even if this American tried to establish blood relative status, it would be extremely difficult not to say expensive to prove any negligence."

"Do we have the gentleman's name?"

"Thomas William Frimble. This is his address."

"Well, I will do some discreet enquiries but I have no qualms in saying to you that you have no worries."

All the chat was related to the others and it was decided to err on the side of caution with the amount of information to be given at this stage. Robert returned with a photographer in the afternoon, took twenty or so stills and left, promising to send copies.

It still gave Isobel uneasy feelings with Robert around but she did not say anything.

All this talk of genealogy had also sparked the imagination of Karen Young. Many times she had thought about where her ancestry lay but never actually done anything.

A few times strange stories had led her quest into background relative situations. It might be fun to look into hers.

First thing she traced was her immediate family tree, her father Arthur Young of Deersholt in Brewald, this took her to the parish records in Melfort. Which was actually Brewald, to find records of a William Young, son of Joshua and Isobel Young nee Hepforth, Keepers Cottage Melfort.

"It couldn't be," she said out loud.

Keeping this close to her chest she wrote to the public records office but the reply stunned her.

It seemed that HER Great grandfather was none other than Joshua Young of Melfort and this was his second wife, the first wife unknown by the records office was apparently dead.

She then wrote to the records office to ask if the first marriage was recorded. There was; his first marriage was registered as being a civil ceremony conducted by the Reverend Domkiss of St Andrews Melfort. Between Joshua Young and Miss Megan Frimble, spinster of this parish. The register had been signed by Derek Frimble and the vicar who had added (in duress) probably after the ceremony.

Having found out that under duress meant a shotgun wedding, it followed that dates had to be important. To her dismay although both marriages were recorded there was no record of either death or burial of this Megan Frimble. Conclusion drawn that he had been a bigamist.

Karen decided to leave the scandal long buried as she was aiming for the very top of her profession which meant she had to have a squeaky-clean scandal free past..

Her feelings were aroused again when she received a letter from a Mr Robert Frimble, from Pittsburgh USA. He had also been bitten by the genealogy bug and had come across information that linked the families of Frimble and Young, however the links were tenuous and not conclusive. Karen replied that she could not confirm or deny any family ties but he may have the wrong Karen Young. Karen was a popular name in Scotland where her mother came from.

Sealing the letter and getting the post girl to frank it with the office stamp gave the letter some authenticity and authority, she thought.

Karen heard no more until one morning her secretary hailed her from the reception. As she entered the reception, she shuddered. She had never met Robert but somehow, she knew who he was.

"Good Morning, Miss Young I believe. I wonder if we might have a word in private, please."

"Certainly, Julia? Is the interview room free."

"Yes, Miss Young for the next hour."

"Then could you show Mr Frimble there and arrange for some coffee, I will be there in a few moments." It gave her a few moments to compose herself.

"Ah, thank you, Julia, make sure we are not disturbed."

"Now, Mr Frimble."

"Robert, please."

"How can I be of assistance?"

"This is all very delicate and unusually personal but are you sure that your heritage is indeed Scottish."

"An impertinent question and very unnerving Mr Frimble."

"I in no way wish to offend but the research I have done leads me to believe that we are indeed related, I also have to accept that records then were not as they are today and this could all be entirely coincidental."

"Mr Frimble… Robert You may or may not be aware that in the judicial hierarchy of this country if anyone is perceived as having a dubious history contrary to public niceties any application to the bar would be frowned upon. As I hope to progress to the bar in the very near future, I would not want my application to be hindered by myths about my history. So, any buried bones, as it were I hoped, would be left buried. Do I make myself clear.?

"Miss Young, I do apologise for the intrusion and I can assure you that any knowledge gained from this exercise is purely to satisfy my and my brothers' curiosity.

If this causes distress for any reason, I assure you that it will cease."

It was two weeks before she heard from him again, in the first instance he sent her a large bouquet and an apology. The second was a phone call… "I hope you enjoyed the flowers."

"They were delightful, Robert but really no need for them or the apology. "

"Indeed, there was, and I am now asking you out to dinner tonight if you will accept."

"Good then I will have the car pick you up at eight."

Right on the dot of eight, a chauffeur rang her doorbell and was about to lead her to the Rolls Royce when he said

"Excuse me madam, please don't think it rude of me but is that the foot attire you intended to be out in?"

She looked down at the pink mule slippers and died on the spot. Two minutes later she was back wearing heel back open toed black shoes and a big blush.

"Very nice, madam."

The car slipped gracefully away into the night to the hotel. In stepped Robert, resplendent in full evening jacket and red cummerbund, "Where are we going?"

Robert had always had a yen to be a James bond and the Brewald hotel was having a bond themed night which was thoroughly enjoyed which included a Bond style casino, at which she won.

She had warmed to him as the night wore on but declined a nightcap, "Pity," he said, "I am back to the states tomorrow."

The following morning, she drove to work and was greeted by Carole the receptionist.

"Some evening then?" she said, smirking.

"What do you mean."

"Open the door."

The smell from the biggest basket of flowers she had ever seen burst through the door.

There was a note in a small envelope.

Karen closed the door and opened the envelope.

'So sorry, please forgive me for getting carried away with the Bond theme.

I hope still your friend Robert XX'

Karen sealed it again and it went into her handbag.

The desk phone rang, "Miss Young, I have a Mr Frimble on the other line."

"Karen, It's Robert I am just about to take off but I…

"Robert, I am so sorry about last night. Thank you for the beautiful flowers."

"Karen, would you mind if I wrote to you from the States?"

"I would be disappointed if you didn't."

Carole came in with the coffee and a knowing look.

How the morning dragged if it were not for Carole keeping her on the straight and narrow, by the time her last appointment had gone she felt quite drained.

"Carole, I have to go on a house visit this afternoon," she said as she left the office which was a euphemism for I am off for the afternoon personal time. It made up for one or two of the nights working.

Sitting in the Pigs Trotters it was known locally, Karen had a long drink in front of her. She definitely felt a stare or two at a lone woman drinking in a pub in an afternoon even in today's 'free society.'

A tall youth took her attention as he walked into the quaint but old fashioned and low beam as he crossed to the bar, replacing the dislodged horse brass clumsily pushed a watch perched on the beam into Karen's lap. The youth saw it had not smashed on the floor and offered to replace it on the beam Karen motioned him away. She was about to hand it back to the barman when she realised a warm feeling emanated from the case that was emotional not physical.

I must get another nail to put in that beam to properly hang Josh's watch. He mumbled.

"Excuse me," she said to the two very old very crusty old men in the corner, "Did the barman just mention the name Josh?"

It was a long time ago that any lady let alone a pretty lady had talked to him and he savoured the puff on his sweet-smelling tobacco, looked her straight in the eye. "That would be Young Josh once a gamekeeper in these parts, he was staring at Karen, "You from these parts."

"No, not really just doing a home visit for a client here."

"You know, begging your pardon ma'am but you remind me of someone," said Jeb.

"Ere, Knocker, do you think this lady reminds you of someone?"

"She bears a striking resemblance to Mary."

"But Mary who?"

"Why, Mary Frimble of course."

"By golly you are right Mary Frimble, thank goodness you have a long memory Knocker."

"I can remember years ago but not yesterday."

"Excuse me gentlemen, but you did say Frimble and why are you called knocker?"

"EE's called knocker cause he was postie here for ever and if anyone wanted to be got up early, he would knock on the door or window for them."

"As to the Frimble story, it be a long and dry one," he said.

She caught the barman's eye and he brought two pints and a gin and lime over.

Curiosity was now at boiling point.

"Now Gentlemen tell me all you know about the Frimbles."

All the way home she could not get out of her head that she was possibly related to these Frimbles and also a distant cousin to Robert. The thought that she had privileged information from a client meant she was duty bound to inform the other clients. She would ask the advice of the senior partner if he was still in his office.

As she entered the senior partners office realising it was bigger than all the rest even though hers was bulging with work. He dispelled her worries and John could take on the Half Moon House case if it should be required and the senior partner could take on the pending case in the meantime.

Funny that the senior partner always seems to get the juicy cases. Perhaps the symbiosis will work in her favour one day.

Duly patted on the head, she returned to her own office having 'done the right thing' but she would have to talk to the Jenkins and the Wardhays. Karen cleared and moved appointments from the following afternoon to give her chance to do a face-to-face chat with the four of them to explain why she could no longer act on their behalf in this matter without their prior consent knowing that she has a personal involvement.

Arriving at the start of the drive, she was impressed from the word go with the sympathetic way they had set about the renovations and the setting in the wood. Although she knew it had been renovated to a high modern standard, she could feel the warmth and love within those renovated walls and the whole thing looked as if it had been built in a different era.

She had thought it might just evoke some feelings within her but it felt like any other home visit where there was business to be concluded. On the other hand, Isobel was absolutely struck dumb when Karen was introduced to the other three by Chris. By the time it came to Issie to shake her hand she had gained her composure somewhat and held out a welcoming hand. The hands entwined and Issie felt a strange warmth, a sensual glow flowing two ways she was sure of it.

But Issie had no way of knowing that Karen felt the same way, no way could she ask her.

Karen HAD felt the same flow of whatever it was but it felt like a family bond between them.

Seconds passed like hours until Chris broke the air and invited Karen to sit down..

When they were all sitting Karen began stone faced. "The reason I am here today is that I can no longer act in your interests in this property."

"Why not?" asked John.

"Simply because I would have to declare an interest in the outcome of the inquiries being made that may indicate that I am one of the surviving members of the Frimble family. This only came to light yesterday by odd chance."

"I knew it," exclaimed Issie.

Karen continued, "In the light of this information and possible proof of kinship I have asked one of our senior partners to act on your behalf if you would so wish."

The other senior partner is as we speak applying to the court for clearance to act on my and my cousin's behalf in the challenge for ownership rights to this property.

"But," started John.

"Please…" said Karen motioning John to hold while she explained, "this does not change any rights that you have with this house or your legal ownership."

"What it does mean is that Robert, James and myself are indeed related to Derek Frimble and will be challenging Lord Pressguard or his estate executors. They will have no alternative but to settle out of court, for reasons I cannot divulge..

"Who are Robert and James "

"They have only been known to us for two or three days as the grandchildren of Thomas William Frimble who apparently was taken in as a foundling by the Allsopp family but subsequently joined a travelling circus or carnival that came to Britain at that time."

"Would you care for a coffee Miss, sorry didn't catch your name."

"Young, but please call me Karen."

"Karen, would you like a coffee."

"Yes, please if it is no trouble."

Matty went off with Issie into the kitchen.

"So, what happens now?" asked Chris.

You and your partners will have to decide if you wish another firm entirely could run the case for you. If you decide to stay with us, we will have two senior partners working on either side with a declaration of known association to avoid any complications. If at any time you are uncomfortable with that you have the right to withdraw from our firm and use another solicitor."

"Can you advise us at all now."

"Strictly off the record it is likely that our senior partner will approach the solicitors dealing with the estate stating the claim. They will ask for evidence that we can provide, we think that a suitable settlement figure will be offered as they would have possibly a long, time-consuming court case which will effectively only mean less money to the treasury as no heirs are known, so it will be easier to settle at that stage".

"How will that affect us here?"

"There will be no change whatsoever, your ownership was never in question as I explained to you in my office."

There was the complication that no deeds were ever made for proof of ownership by Derek Frimble it was just a gentleman's agreement and 25 years of non-usage etc the estate took back the house and grounds as squatters right. That was never registered either but the estate solicitors cannot prove this.

"That's why the deeds to this place put us as second owners only."

"That is right but when Robert came to the office tracing his family tree the first document signing over the property to Derek Frimble was found in our vault, but his Lordship never signed it and it was worthless.

If the estate solicitors don't play ball as I am sure they will because they will not want a protracted law case then we may have to follow a different tack and that would involve you and our involvement with you would have to cease." she smiled. "In this case we have the law on our side because they will want payment for their services that have already incurred and will not want to wait another five or ten years of litigation and no payment."

"After the coffee, I would love to see what you have done here." They showed her round everywhere and explained that there were so many people interested in seeing the house and how it was built. That they were going to flag the inner circle first to provide an outside seating area and the build. Maybe at the same time more of the round house to accommodate a coffee shop and craft room.

Matty and Issie had been busy with needles and thread. Covering chair bottoms and making curtains as well as decorating, they had also redecorated what had become known as Megan's room and replaced the table and chair putting the rusted old typewriter as a centrepiece. As they walked around the house, Karen noticed the steps down to the doorway and asked what that was about.

It's a secret room that we believe was like a priest hole but more for the 'banished young girl' and that was where the foundation of the body in the wall stories seemed to have derived from. Not factually correct but it attracts lots of people wanting to see the haunted room. Karen asked to go in.

"What is this?" she said picking up the white shawl.

"You can see it."

"Of course," she said wrapping it around her shoulders, as she did the clothes she was wearing disappeared and she sat in the corner on a stool not the chair that had rotted away. Matty leaned forward to grasp her arm but Issie stopped her, Karen started to type at the supposedly-stuck typewriter furiously with two fingers. This went on for two or three minutes and then just as quickly as it started, she got up, removed the shawl and all her clothing had returned.

"There is a funny smell in here," Karen was completely unaware of what had just happened.

"Probably the dampness in the soil walls," said Issie, quick thinking as ever.

They were waving her off when Matty said, "She is related you know."

"How can you know that?" said John.

"Woman's intuition."


"Carole, could you come in please."

Carole knew there was something odd she had said please.

"Ah Carole, this may seem strange to you but do we have a client called Mike by any chance?"

"Michael Osborn, the registrar."

"No, he is either Michael or Mr Osborn."

"Michael Firenti, the Artist."

"No. He is called Mick."

"The only other one that come to mind is Michael Thrapston the Butcher."

"No, he is another Mick."

"Is there a reason Miss Young?"

"No. Not really. It's just the name keeps popping up in my mind and I can't put a face to it and yet it feels important."

"No offence, but don't eat cheese late at night."

"Perhaps you are right Carole that's all for now, although could you manage a cup of coffee, please?"

There was that word again. Carole could not believe that Karen did not remonstrate in her usual manner that this is not a music hall and all these pleases. Where has Miss young gone or perhaps been. She smiled.

Karen sat staring at the 'Founder' picture on the wall in front of her but her mind was elsewhere; she drifted off into the dream that had haunted her the last couple of days.

There was woodland all around and a tall handsome man in his twenties in front of her, she knew him but the face had a permanent haze in her eyes. He offered a hand and they walked on through the bluebells and wood anemones.

"Are you alright?" The voice startled her.

She was awoken by Carole gently tapping her shoulder, "Are you okay, only you look as though you have seen a ghost."

"Yes, thank you, Carole, I must have nodded off, did not have a very good night last night."

"You have Mr Robinson in reception to see you about finalising on his house in Trencham."

"Give me a couple of minutes and then show him in, oh and another cup please."

Another please, either she is ill or in love!!

All through the day Karen felt out of control but managed to keep it together. The urge to go back to The Half Moon House was so compelling but she really had no possible excuse for going, by the time the last client of the day had gone she knew she had to go no matter what. In half an hour she was in and out of Melfort on a country road and noticed a heady scent of ah yes bluebells, they were all around her in the woodland, just as in her dream. A tractor and trailer turned onto the road in front of her, and knowing there was absolutely no chance of passing it, she pulled into a field gateway. The handbrake clicked on and the key turned off the engine. In seconds she lost all inhibitions and thoughts of work. She was dancing in the meadow in the lush spring grass.

The tall copse in the distance had a trail leading to it where sheep and deer had trodden for years. Karen was skipping along the trail without a care in the world.

Deeper into the wood she found a glade with a fog like haze hanging in between tree tops. With a figure of a man, she assumed was smoking a pipe, as she moved towards the figure it moved away, she called out but no one heard. The figure emerged back into the sunlight from the copse and was gone. What did this all mean or had she been dreaming again. Clambering over the fence she got to the car and started for

Half Moon House convinced that the secret lay there with the four of them.

Matty was titivating around newly planted shrubs and was not at all surprised to see Karen.

"Hello, Miss Young."

"Mrs Jenkins, forgive the intrusion but I have to speak to someone at this house, I am not sure who or even why but perhaps one of you could unravel the mystery that is haunting me."

"Come in Miss Young, Issie and I are the only ones here at the moment but perhaps we can help."

Karen told them of the dreams and the visit to the copse and the strange feelings she had.

Matty looked at Isobel and they knew that she had a right to know all but how could they convince Chris and John that she was genuine.

Karen looked at Matty, "Do you know who Mike is."

Matty went white and Isobel shuddered.

"How do you come by that name?"

"I don't know why but after the dream I had last night the name is so familiar but I cannot remember ever knowing anyone by that name."

They asked Karen if she would come back later that night and have a meal with them. They had information but it was right that Chris and John should be there.

She agreed and left with all sorts of feelings and also misgivings that might rattle a few skeletons in her cupboard.

John and Chris were on a show and tell, having been to an auction where there were pieces of brassware highly suitable for their cottages or more for the tearooms that they had not built yet.

"You can't let bargains like this slip by." Laughed Chris.

"Well said," Isobel, "While you two have been gadding about the country, finding pubs we have had a visitor."

Chris and John sat down and listened carefully as to what was said.

"We have to be cautious and I think we either tell all or very little."

"But she knows about Mike and the only people who know about him are us four, especially about where he is."

"And there is another thing, while we were showing her around here, she had an experience."

"What kind of experience?"

"She put that shawl and she could see it, on her shoulders and had a similar reaction with the typewriter just as Issie did that first time."

"You mean she was naked and we didn't see," said John.

"And she typed even though it is seized up as you know."

"But we never told her about it."

"Well, if we all agree," said Chris. "We have to tell her everything "

Unanimously all hands went up. All with the realisation that this could go horribly wrong for them.

When Karen arrived, she was feeling equally as uneasy about hearing things that might change the course of her life forever or maybe it was all tales unsubstantiated, that would remain as myths in the annals of time.

Polite niceties were made and Karen asked about the rhomboid shape of the rooms.

"You get used to them after a while," said Matty. The only thing we would change if we go further is to make the windows larger to be able to see more of the view especially on a sunny day, but we kept to the original as much as possible.

"Still very pleasant though," said Karen.

"You must be wondering why we asked you over tonight," Issie was ladeling out proudly from the vegetable soup all from the new garden.

"Well, I am intrigued," said Karen.

"Please, you don't need to frown, there is nothing that is unpleasant, just delicate and sometimes difficult to put into words. And please, we have to ask you to divorce yourself from your legal position in all this. This is more difficult for us as you will find out, but before that, friends, I will ask you to raise a glass to our first guest in our new house. 'Karen'."

There were the usual sorts of tales of mishaps during the build and how John thought he had ordered a couple of bags of manure and ended up with five tons of the smelly stuff on the front drive. The single wheeled barrow was well used for three days. And when Matty went to the DIY shop to get a left-handed screwdriver, which the assistant clued up to and wrapped it. When Matty realised there was absolutely no difference, well you can imagine..

Karen was feeling quite at home and relaxed by the time the real talking started.

Chris had been elected to relate the story as best as possible knowing there may be interjections by the other three.

"You will have to be quite attentive and no doubt will want to ask questions but please try not to interrupt what even to us will seem an incredulous story.

Karen listened intently as Chris related the story, even Issie joined her, absolutely dumbstruck all the way through. Chris did not tell her about the jewellery at this stage.

"So, you see, what a quandary this puts us in."

"Let's get one thing out of the way, this is all strictly off the record and I am not going to give advice. My statement to you about your ownership etc still stands. The only thing I have to do as an interested party is to inform, with your explicit consent, Robert and his twin brother in the states. I think he and I have formed a friendship and I also think he wants to tell stories of daring do, to his kids whenever. He is not looking for anything but information."

They invited Karen to stay the night as they had been drinking, she accepted. It gave them a lot more time to chat and for Karen to ask questions.

During that night they heard a scream and went out onto the patio to see Karen apparently trying to drag something across the floor.

She had no clothes on and Chris was told to fetch a blanket and some slippers but be quiet as she thought Karen was talking and walking in her sleep.

Chris dashed into the room grabbed a blanket and slippers, he threw the blanket over her slim shoulders and carefully assisted by Issie now put the slippers on her bleeding feet. Karen was crying into Matty's shoulder as they walked her slowly back to the bedroom, "It's over now," said Matty, comforting her as she put her into the bed where she fell fast asleep. "I'll stay here in the wicker chair just in case she has the urge to go out again." Chris fetched another blanket and placed it over Matty in the wicker chair.

Next morning, Karen woke up with a tickly blanket around her in a strange room, her head ached and her feet hurt.

"Thought you might like a cup of tea," said Matty.

"Thank you, but what am I doing here?"

"What do you remember of last night?"

"I remember going to bed and, wait a minute, there was someone outside being attacked it seemed so vivid and I can't remember clearly." Beads of sweat appeared on her brow.

"Chris and I found you outside sleepwalking. We brought you back to bed for safety and I stopped here with you."

"How embarrassing, was I…like this…

"Morning Miss Young, I hope you are feeling alright this morning, I brought you some cream and bandages if necessary for your feet," he said quite matter of fact. "Would you care for some breakfast?"

"It seems I owe you an apology for last night," Karen said sheepishly.

"No bother I assure you." His thoughts were, with that body you can disturb me anytime but he could feel Matty's disapproval.

"Now breakfast?"

"Just some toast and coffee if it is no trouble, please."

"We have some croissant if you would prefer."

"Oh, lovely, thanks."

After breakfast it was said that John knew nothing of the night's exploits and nothing would be told, Karen nodded her gratitude.

"So where do we go from here?" asked John.

"Please, I have no wish to cause any disharmony here but I must talk to Robert and his brother in America, to gauge their view, I am sure they will have questions as do I but nothing to change your situation here and no unnecessary expense. I may invite them over and they may have some questions for you directly."

When Karen had left, they convened to discuss it all. Did they need to get another solicitor, should they continue to befriend Karen, should they inform her of the jewel situation. After much discussion about ethics and morals they eventually decided to befriend Karen and the two brothers, say nothing about the jewels and wait.

"Hi Karen, I got your message, I am in Sheffield next Wednesday, can we meet?"

"Certainly, give me a ring when you are here?"

First, she had to listen to advice from Sir Henry, second ignore it. Thirdly, to gather all the evidence she could to corroborate Robert's evidence and prepare to present it. Fourthly she convinced herself that she needed a couple of new outfits… just for business of course.

"Carole."

"Yes, Miss Young."

"What appointments have I got for this afternoon?"

Only Mr Shaw coming in to sign the house documents, he will be here in ten minutes.

"Good, can you register me out for the rest of the afternoon please and take messages for tomorrow morning please."

There was the word again, it is love.

"Yes Miss Young, err Mr Shaw has arrived shall I call for Mr Dawn to come up to witness the signature, and will you be needing me as well?"

"Yes, please Carole."

Contract duly signed and witnessed Mr Shaw was ushered out quite quickly in comparative terms Karen left for the day. This was a strange experience for her, normally she would be looking for business suits but somehow, she was feeling more adventurous and daring.

She eventually narrowed the search to a two piece from Sparks. A flowery dress from Lady Mogs, an evening dress from Dirhams and a rather trendy trouser suit from Griswolds, what a name for a couture shop. that would cover all bases.

She thought about matching things but then a thought struck her. What if he was married, it had never been mentioned.

When her phone rang, she was between clothes and looking into her full-length mirror at various lumps and bumps in all the wrong places.

"Hi Robert, yes of course, oh you can't be here on Wednesday. Never mind, another time. WHAT? The line is crackling, you are here tonight instead? Where, oh yes, I know it. I will see you there in half an hour."

That was the wake-up call. She quickly jumped into the bath and was ready in thirteen minutes flat.

She arrived at the restaurant all calm and serene but realised she had no make up on at all.

She decided to bluff her way through.

Robert had ordered a table but was a little late but the waiter showed her to the table and offered to bring her a drink. She sat there like a dummy for half an hour but he did turn up most apologetic, blaming his boss.

"Never mind, was it a useful meeting, "

"Not really, he just fired me, brought me all this way just to fire me."

"Would you like to call this evening off."

"Hell no, they are paying for my stay here and it will be fun I hope."

She took the bull by the horns. "Do you want to phone your brother and your wife?"

"Nah James has pinched the job and I am not married, whoever told you that."

"Sorry, I just assumed…" She blushed. "What about your job?"

"At my level it is a natural hazard, I can get a job back in the states easily and with a big payoff and a private pension with possibly a golden hello I will be fine, now let's eat."

"I was more bothered that I would not be able to be here on pretence and you would send me away."

"Why would I do that, and we do have some business here." She turned towards him and they kissed. The relationship passed budburst.

In the morning after breakfast at the hotel she brought him up to speed with all the happenings at The Half Moon House including her acceptance of an agreement with the four.

"Well, I would agree with all that, I would love to see the property. Do you think they would mind?"

I get the feeling that they would love to see you. I also think there is a lot more to the story that they are not telling but that is my solicitor's nose, they have been very kind to me."

"That's good enough for me then I will follow your lead."

"I will arrange a meeting with them for tomorrow if you are to stay here."

"Great, I think I can afford a hotel for a night or two." He winked.

When Karen arrived at the office, Carole waved a message to her. She was to go up to Sir Henry straight away.

The tedious way one had to climb stairs to his office was archaic especially as he had his own private lift up to it. still when she became head of chambers, she would have that changed.

Sir Henry was with someone else.

"Ah Miss Young let me introduce Sir Peter Fortescue Brown of Pequins, Pequins and Pequins."

*Another fuddy duddy well past his sell by date*, thought Karen as he offered a hand of friendship

She shook the limp fish and let it go back to its pond.

"Now," said Sir Henry, "It seems Peter and I have been blessed with the role of arbiters in the matter between yourself, The Frimble brothers and the Pressguard estate. As such are you able to speak for the two brothers and yourself."

"There are no signed instructions but yes I am."

"As such are you prepared to put your cards on the table."

"If you mean am I prepared to discuss the substantial evidence that we have obtained for disclosure should this go to a court then I would have to say firmly but politely NO."

"Quite," said Sir Peter.

Sir Henry looked over his half glasses and asked if a solution could be found to satisfy this thirst for knowledge. Are you in a position to act for the other two parties and yourself? The other party can be contacted within the hour and a decision formed.

"Very well, Sir Henry, could I ask you just to step out for a few moments whilst I have an off the record chat with Miss Young."

"Highly irregular old boy, but in the circumstances, perhaps wise."

*************************

Robert, do you know the coffee shop on the corner of Bakewell Street in Melfort?"

"Meet me there in ten minutes."

"No buts."

"Okay."

Karen greeted Robert extremely formally and explained that you never know who is watching.

They had two cups of steaming coffee.

"What is so urgent?"

"Has James enabled you to make any decision on his behalf with regards to this possible court case."

"Actually, I have here a piece of paper saying exactly that, he signed it before I left but not dated.

"Good and are you both willing for me to negotiate on your behalf."

"Yes."

"Well, it has been offered to me that if we accepted the sum of two hundred and fifty thousand pounds each and there was no more talk of litigation or investigation. The whole matter can be resolved by midday today."

Robert was spluttering coffee.

"Pounds Sterling," he said.

"You will have to sign a paper that says you will have no more involvement with any litigation in regards to any property on the Lord Pressguard estate…"

"I was only curious in the first place, so no problem and thank you so much for handling the proposition."

"Well, I can now tell you that we have not accepted the two hundred and fifty thousand, I negotiated for five hundred thousand each in cash on completion of the signatures.

"Well done …you are really something."

"I will take that as a compliment."

"By the way, that meeting this morning is and won't be documented nor will any outcome the matter stops today. Is that clearly understood?"

"Yes Ma'am.|" Curiosity was dripping from every pore on his body.

At twelve o'clock, they were carrying three bearer bonds totalling 1,000000 pounds to the nearest bank.

They had the manager in a bit of a spin, he had not handled such bonds before.

The bank minions sorted the validity and transfer to Robert and James in America. They also opened an account in Karen's name for her ten per cent.

The hotel porter had been asked for strange things in his time but never enough champagne to fill a double bath and a large tray of strawberries. Mine not to reason why. It had been a wild dream of Roberts that if he was ever rich enough, he would enjoy such a luxury.

Karen rang the office and disposed of her appointments to her assistant Matthew and laid back in the warm champagne and sucked the strawberries. The rats in the hotel sewers would be drunk as skunks that night.

Over an indulgent smoked salmon breakfast Robert let curiosity get the better of him.

"Why would the Pressguard estate pay out so much money without too much trouble?

Karen looked very firmly at him. "I told you I cannot reveal the answer to that question and secondly you cannot ask any questions at all, both morally and legally, so shut up and eat your toast. All I can say is there was a very good reason. "

"How about we pop over to see the four musketeers at Half Moon House today. They can show me the house properly."

"If you like, although I get creepy feelings going into the house."

As Karen's car pulled up at the Half Moon, gate a chill swept over Matty,

"She is here again."

"Who?"

"That Karen girl."

"How do you know that."

"Because I can see her car in the mirror at the gate."

"You sent shivers up and down my spine then."

"I wonder what she wants now "

"Perhaps to live here." Matty and Issie turned round to the voice to see no one.

Karen knocked at the door.

"Did you hear something then/"

"No, did you?"

They both looked at the piece of paper that floated from the ceiling as it slowed to a halt the knock on the door came again...

Karen and Robert were invited in. There were fresh scones and jam on the table.

"Good news, the estate solicitors have capitulated completely and have decided to settle out of court. Robert, his brother and I have been paid off without going to court at all."

"How does that affect us?" asked Matty with more than a tinge of fear in her voice.

Nothing will change here the estate will sweep under the carpet any happenings or malpractices for ever. A piece of white paper was swept up in a draft and a chill went down Issie's back. Karen also appeared to shrug off the chill.

"Matty, why do I always get the impression that there is something I should know when I come here." The direct question took Matty off-guard for a moment enough for the courtroom diva to pounce. "So, there is something in the depths of this place. She was like a lion stalking its prey and ready to pounce any time.

"Anything that has happened in the past is our concern alone," was her defence..

"She is right you know," said Robert in Matty's defence.

"I am sorry I didn't mean to offend or upset anyone. I guess it is my instinct for my job. I apologise."

Just then the two lads came in holding a glass box with a stuffed mounted fox "a bargain for three quid."

"You two should hold each other's hands at these sorties then you would not buy such rubbish at antiques fairs."

"It will look good on the mantelpiece over the fire."

"It will look better on the fire, it is a poor dead animal OUT OUT."

John made a whimper like a dog and left the room with the glass box and contents but was allowed back.

Karen and Robert have come to inform us that there will be no court case over the property or any other matters referring to the Pressguard estate.

"What happened," said Chris.

"The solicitors made an offer we could not refuse so we didn't..

"So, what happens now," said Issie.

"Well, for a start let's crack open a bottle."

"Er, do you have anything other than Champagne," said Robert had had a surfeit.

"Oh," said Chris with a wink, "perhaps a gentle white wine from the cool rack."

He came back with a tray and six glasses. All ready to wet the whistles.

"If I may," said Robert, "I would love to see the house now that you have completed your renovations."

"Of course, but it will be a long time before it is all completed. Come on Chris, let's leave the gossip to the girls and talk man stuff."

"So, what's the story then?" Issie was looking at Karen straight in the eye.

"What?"

"Oh, come on, it is seen a mile away, dish the dirt what's between you and Robert."

"We…"

"I knew it, the glow, the holding hands and sitting so close together." Issie was relentless.

"Is it that obvious?" blushed Karen.

"They are smashing people," said Robert as they drove away."

"Intuitive as well they had us sussed straight away ," said Karen;

"Is there an us?"

"I hope so." She looked into his starry blue eyes. The trip home seemed ever so short they neither could get home fast enough to enjoy each other's uninterrupted company.

The next morning, life brought them from the clouds. More mundane matters like how long could Robert stay, did Karen want to continue working considering her new found wealth.

He looked her straight in the eyes and ignoring her breakfast attire and unkempt hair, "Karen, the last time I went back to the states I promised myself that should I have the opportunity I would use it to tell you that I love you more than words can express and if you feel as I do?"

"I do."

"Then Miss Young, would you please do me the great honour of becoming my wife."

"That won't do, come on, one knee and all that." She was laughing.

"Yes, Mr Robert Frimble, I love you too and yes I will marry you."

"And can we now or as we will be, a millionaire family, get a more comfortable bed, it may be suitable for one but not sumptuous for two.

"What millionaire family? Oh yes, we will be. How about we spend some of it today in town."

"Before all that I have been thinking while staring at your cracked ceiling."

"Careful, that's the family brain cell you are using." She smoothed his brow.,

"Seriously, I don't know about you but every time I go to The Half Moon House I am almost magnetised to stay there as though I actually belong."

"Well, funny you should say that, I always feel it is quite a magical place and special."

"The first time I visited I knew I would have to return, for no reason but a feeling of compulsion to go back."

Karen had the same feelings, she explained to him that she also had strange but kind feelings there just like it was a family home where she felt warm and cosy.

He gazed in admiration as she stood in front of the full-length mirror deciding which outfit to wear.

"The pink," he said, "makes you look all girly and pretty."

"I have to go to the office just once to clear things up and instruct Matthew, details of clients and such."

"How long will you be out of sight?"

"A couple of hours tops."

"Could I borrow your car for a while, something I have to do."

"Yes, drop me off at the office and pick me up later when you are done."

They showered and dressed, had a leisurely breakfast and then went.

Robert waved. "Pick you up around twelve thirty."

His thoughts turned to earlier in the day as he drove to the Half Moon House.

He needed a little alone time to think it through so stopped in a gateway and parked up.

The field was empty with no sheep or cattle and obviously the grass had been taken away. He watched as two or three rabbits played along the hedgerow and noticed three straight trunked trees on the other side of the field and in a few moments, he was sitting at the base of one of them collecting his thoughts. All he could think about was how to approach the four knowing his yearning to live in the house. As he rose, he grasped at the tree where a large burr stuck out covering some sort of injury in its earlier life. He had an urge to carve the bark above it and could just make out a large M in the centre of the burr scar. The K was relatively easy and he stood back to admire his handiwork but felt the hard round barrels of a shotgun at his back.

"I…" started Robert.

"I. Will give you just ten seconds to get back over there to your car and bugger off or I will start shooting."

Robert was not waiting to argue. His heart thumping waiting for the shot got to the gate and cleared it. He looked back across the field there was nothing, no one and in the distance shining white was a K on the trunk. He now had every sympathy with the fox in the glass case and swore if he ever could he would ban shooting on the land.

Back at the office Karen had spoken to Matthew and Carole, said her goodbyes and was about to leave when Sir Henry emerged from his lift. "Ah Karen, my dear, so sorry to lose you, er could I have a word in your old office please."

"I have known Sir Peter for seventy odd years, and have never known him cave in like the other day over any lawsuit. How did you manage it?"

"Well Sir Henry, have you ever noticed that Sir Peter has quite a birthmark on his shoulder and neck? I noticed it when he bent down to pick up some papers. All I said to him was that there were bound to be paternity and maternity tests involved with the whole case and maybe he should be tested as well.”

“You clever girl!”

At Half Moon House, Robert found John pottering, “I hope you don’t mind me calling unannounced but is it possible to have a word with you all.”

“Sounds like a reasonable excuse to stop weeding, come in.”

“Robert would like a serious word with us about something. Is Chris about?”

“He’ll be back in a minute Coffee anyone?”

Chris came in. “Does not take much of a coffee smell to stop you weeding.” He laughed.

“Oh, hello Robert. I did not know you were here. Are you alright? You look a little peaky.

“Just had a bit of a run in with the gamekeeper who took a dislike to where I was sitting minding my own business over those three big trees. I got the impression he thought I was someone else but with a twelve bore-in hand, I was not arguing. Do you happen to know what the M carved in the tree is all about?

It was Chris’s turn to turn pale.

“Anyway, I came to see you, not the local vigilantes.”

This may seem very strange to you, but both Karen and I and there is to be a Karen and I, feel that this is just like home to us. It’s warm and cosy and feels somehow right. If that makes sense.” Robert noticed looks being thrown between the four.

“Now don’t worry we are not about to run you out of town but I have a notion that you might consider. Please bear in mind that Karen knows nothing of my coming here today.”

"We are all ears," said Matty.

How would you feel about completing this house as it was first intended by filling in the missing half in exactly the same build that you have here now and at our expense?"

Chris, ever cautious, "Where exactly would the money come from?"

"Both Karen and I have considerable assets due to a recent deal so there is no problem there as far as money is concerned. I started by saying that this COULD be a project if you agreed but I have not said anything to Karen so if your feeling is a definite *No*, then this is where it ends."

"We would have to have serious words first."

"Of course, but if I now broach the subject with Karen and she is for it, please don't upset my apple cart by telling her I have already spoken to you."

"We understand completely," said Matty, "Why don't you come over tonight, we will have a barbecue we can discuss then and if all fails, we will still have a good time."

The evening was a huge success and the prior talks between the four were promising.

"I think it would be a good time," said John nudging.

"Err yes, Karen just to make it official and out in the open. Will you marry me?" He held out a ring.

"Yes."

The hushed crowd turned their attention to the burning flesh on the barbecue.

"There is something else Karen." Robert was not quite so confident of an amicable reply.

I had thought the other day at the office and wondered if it was possible and these good folk agreed. How would you feel about completing the circle with this house and making it a FULL Moon House?

"I'd be over the moon, I wouldn't care where we were I would be happy but here would be idyllic.

If it can be all worked out.

John coughed to say we are here and the discussions went on into the night. agreements were settled and they agreed to allow Robert and Karen to apply for planning consent so long as all fees were paid by them. There were the original plans but no tea shop. Plenty of room for another family especially as the original idea was that Kevin would come back.

"It will take a while to build," said Matty.

"I have an idea there," said Robert. "Why don't we leave you with enough money to get materials and builders?" I could wind up our affairs in America.

"How many affairs are there?" laughed Karen.

"Would you allow Chris and I to do the main building?"

"Looking at your previous exploits I have no qualms about that."

"Great, we needed a project to work on."

With no taxi available to take them home and the booze having flowed quite readily the offer of a safe bed was accepted.

They were soon sound asleep in the warmth and depth of the down mattresses and hardly moved until the sun managed to force its way through a chink in the curtain.

When Karen was fully awake, she pulled back the curtains and could see Chris weeding in the corner vegetable patch. Karen moved to wave, then realised she actually had no clothes on yet and changed her mind. Robert just caught sight of her going round the corner of the shower and decided to join her. Having heard them moving around Issie had brunch ready and the two of them followed their noses to the kitchen.

"Good morning, sleep well?"

"Heavenly, that bed is wonderful. When your son comes home it will be seventh heaven for him."

*If ever*, thought Matty.

John and Chris made the frame, Matty and I took a little trip up north and got the down from just over the Scottish border. We bought the duvets and covers from the local market in Melfort.

"This could be so wonderful, tell me, last night wasn't a dream?" said Robert absolutely straight faced.

"No, not a dream here. I'll pinch you just in case."

Later in the day Robert left a Cheque for two hundred thousand pounds as a deposit and materials budget with a power of attorney letter should they need it at the council.

"When shall we get married?"

"Should we wait until after we get back from America then your relatives can come."

"There are none left to invite now," he said with quite a dark inflection in his voice.

"What about yours here?"

"There are none I would want to invite except the Half Moonies."

"Then let's arrange for a registrar and keep it simple."

"Why a registrar? Matty knows a Vicar who I am sure would love to officiate."

"Great, let's get the details sorted. I can have whatever papers we need sent over from the states."

"I am sure the steeple fund could do with a boost."

"That Roger is really something, modern thinking and a heart of gold, he would like you to go over to the church this afternoon and arrange things for say a month from now to allow time for all the correct paperwork to be sorted. Karen left a hefty donation regardless of Rogers insistence that it was really not required."

"All set then the date and the start on the house, Issie and Matty would arrange for caterers to cope with 24 people at the Half Moon House."

Chris had spoken to a couple of 'friends' at the council and the work could start straight away.

Karen had sent invites to office people and arranged for the flowers in the church and a small posy for her to carry.

A wedding dress was being fitted on her return and transport was to be a traditional pony and trap.

Robert had asked both John and Chris to be his best men and Sir Henry would give Karen away.

All organised, they went off to the states.

Unbeknown to Robert and Karen, Chris had arranged for an advert in the paper asking for volunteers to work on a conservation project and had fourteen replies already in. They had to go with modern construction in foundations but concrete was soon swirling into place. Stone arrived, Purlins and joists were delivered and tiles organised from another site were being stacked carefully ready for use when the time was right. They had volunteers from all over eager to learn the skills of this type of unusual build. John and Chris ran the build day to day but not as much hands on as they would have liked.

On one particular day the postie came with a letter from the council with the planning consent to build. Phew. The walls were already up to scaffold height, and the next layer was under way.

Kingpins queen posts nibs mitre joints and noggins were all holding the purlins and joists in their rightful places and all as if by magic and planning the window frames arrived.

They were six weeks into the build and wondering where the money would come from to finish the project when a sleek black Daimler Sovereign pulled onto the drive. A bronzed Karen got out from one side, open mouthed at the progress and Robert climbed out of the other taking in the site before him. "Wow, I have seen them build fast in the states but you two take the prize."

"Well, the amount of tea consumed by various building inspectors from all over the place has been a slowing down factor, generally they have been a hindrance."

"But how did you manage to get so far so quickly?

"Watch."

He blew a whistle and workmen came pouring out what will be the coffee shop as planned There were also two women amongst them obviously builders in boiler suits.

The leader that came out said it wasn't time to start but Chris apologised and asked them to meet the new co- owners and future occupiers.

"How is the budget?" asked Robert.

"With all the speed, it is all accounted for; but we will need more to complete, the sparks are due to first fix tomorrow and the plasterers and plumbers the week after so a cheque would be welcome."

"You four are absolutely the best," said Karen.

"There you are," Robert handed another cheque. "I don't think we will be needing this much but we are keeping count so…"

"Who is keeping count?" said Matty deftly, sweeping the cheque from Chris's builder's hands.

"Matty is keeping accounts," he said sheepishly.

With the wedding just three weeks away and all organised, Karen dropped in at the office to drop off the official invites which was a rather poor excuse for showing off her engagement ring of a large emerald surrounded by diamonds and all set-in white gold. When Sir Henry got wind of the fact that KAREN who also happened now to be one of their esteemed clients was in the building came down on his lift to reception.

"Ah Miss Young, please come into the main office. Now I hear the wedding arrangements are all in place."

"Yes, Sir Henry and you remember you kindly consented to giving me away."

"I did. you will have to remind my secretary where and what time." She was beginning to regret the offer but at least he would go soon after the ceremony.

"Now must dash. I have furniture to arrange and buy." He could not avoid the handshake this time and for her it was a little stronger than normal.

Robert had been driving Chris and John nuts disturbing the normally quiet and steady workforce and generally getting under everybody's feet, when he disappeared in his sleek car, they sighed with relief.

"I now know what it must have been like when I visited sites in the past."

"Yep, a right royal pain in the ass." Laughed John. Despite several bouts of interference, the build was on schedule the wedding plans in place the honeymoon booked in Paris and the housewarming when the house was complete. Furniture was arriving during the week they were away. The banns had been read no one seemed to be aware or concerned at the association with the Frimble name and the Young name on the same sheet of paper.

Roger read the banns for the last time and in the vestry afterwards he and his wife were invited to the reception at the now Whole Moon House.

The day approached quite rapidly but on Friday, there was a huge storm with lots of lightning strikes. No one in living memory had seen a storm like it and the Pigs Trotter pub was destroyed by the lightning and all-consuming fire. People were fearing for their lives and waited for the huge deluge expected to follow the light display but none came. The street lighting was restored to normal and people gingerly ventured back onto the street, only to see the single fire tender damping down the pub.

Next day was totally different. The sun was shining. The birds were twittering, even a lonely skylark rose from the cornfield to tell the story of how it meets its mate getting higher and higher.

John and Chris were up with that lark checking for loose or slipped tiles. "Nothing out of place here," said John. They decided to check inside the 'OTHER HALF' as they were now calling it.

John turned the key in the large Victorian lock of the impressive panelled oak door they had managed to buy second hand and refurbished, "that was a very good buy."

"Right, you go left and I will go right."

All okay.

Breakfast was next on the agenda. The sun shone the whole day, it was smiles all round.

When the congregation watched the bride enter and walk up the aisle, John was deputising for Sir Henry as he had ducked out of the duty. The scene was set with Chris and John flanking the bride and groom.

Dearly beloved we are gathered .....................

Isobel nudged Matty.

"Do you see what I see," they were whispering.

"I think so, do you think anyone else can?"

As the groom stood side by side there was a veiled fuzzy light and stood side by side behind them two completely naked people. Standing hand in hand draped only in a flimsy see-through white shroud it was so sheer that it was quite clear what gender they were.

Roger seemed oblivious to the apparitions and was continuing the service. John and Chris were forwards of them and would not be looking back. Roger continued; I, Robert Derek take thee Karen Mary to be…

Matty stifled a scream successfully whispering to Issie, "Robert DEREK and Karen MARY!"

"Dear God, what have we done,'' Issie whispered. They watched as the two apparitions followed everything in the service. As if in a trance they watched as the two figures exchanged rings and walked down the aisle looking only at each other no one in the pews seemed to see anything of what was happening The two reached the porch door and just walked straight through it with a little wave.

"Issie, Matty. The register?" was the muffled cry as Chris was motioning them to go up to sign,

Issie looked at Matty and vice versa. They walked up to the table and signatures were put on the register. Two bells rang the best they could to tell the world there had been a wedding.

Back at the FULL MOON HOUSE which they actually still called the Half Moon House, speeches were short and to the point. Best man speech was a toast to the bride and Groom then Robert got up to say all the thank yous for all the presents and cards and a special thank you to the *Four*, without whom none of this would have been possible and finally two toasts one to my wife and two to friendships we hope will never end. Glasses were chinked and the party was in full swing, it was only when Robert and Karen were about to leave to go to Paris when he asked for quiet as he had some news. "I can't keep this quiet any longer, and now we are married. I can tell you that in the next few months there will be the pitter patter of tiny feet in 'The Other Half.'

Ladies and Gentlemen please be upstanding for THE BABY..

He kissed Karen saying I love you and they left for Paris.

A little while later Issie and Matty got the two lads together in the tea room and told them what they had witnessed in the church and no they had not touched a drop at that stage. There was also something they might have seen earlier. All the three chestnut trees were lying on the ground obviously struck by the lightning.

"How do you know it was them at the altar?"

"How many Dereks and Marys do you know," scolded Matty.

"How do you mean the names were the same?"

The second name of Robert was Derek and Karen's was Mary, the vicar said them and they were repeated.

Chris held Matty's arm and John held Isobel's.

Those names were NEVER spoken in the church today.

"Are you saying that no one heard or saw anything out of the ordinary today?

Matty felt the cold chill again, "We need to see the register, NOW!"

The four drove to the church and strangely the door was open, the pews were empty and no sign of Roger. The late sun was shining on the brass at the altar and on the stained-glass window with light dancing over the floor as the clouds moved.

"Hello, can I help?" Thinking they had left something behind.

The voice sent chills up and down.

"Over here, just changing the hymn numbers."

The hairs settled; it was Roger.

"Er Roger, could we ask a small favour?"

"After the donation today, how could I refuse?"

"Could we look at the register please?"

"Can you tell me why?"

"Not really."

"I will have to be with you and no photos can be taken."

The Book was brought from the vault and opened on the polished oak desk.

The light went on and Matty turned a couple of pages. Look there on the age worn page was the entry the marriage between DEREK FRIMBLE AND MARY YOUNG of this parish Sept 28th 1887.

"Perhaps you can tell me now."

"Just a minute, Roger." She turned the page for today it just said Robert and Karen.

Back at the vicarage for yet more hot chocolate, they describe the happening of the day and all the coincidences.

"This little old parish certainly packs a few choice punches, bringing colour into our lives."

"The thing is he went on all I can do is to make a note of all that has happened and wait until it may or not be needed, no one has been harmed and there appear to be no evil spirits at work."

"Thank you for your hospitality and advice. You really must come over to us one evening, bring Mrs Roger," invited Matty.

"Thank you for bringing some real-life changing moments to me. It creates an intriguing picture in an otherwise ordinary parish."

The Four walked back to the car with a definite feeling of being watched. Walked over to the church and lynch gate as they turned the corner to go through the gate there was a creamy glow from the moon and a small whitish light inside the gated area.

Two figures in silhouette confronted them. There were no movements from the spot but a voice had them spellbound and riveted to the spot.

"Friends, fear nothing you have helped our daughter in her plight. Now you have the opportunity to stop it happening again. In your hearts and hands lie her destiny. HELP THE NEW MEGAN."

There was little significance in what was said and no one really knew who had said it or what sense it made.

The Four continued with their quest to get the other half totally finished before Robert and Karen came home from their honeymoon. With all the wonderful volunteer help it was just in need of a few finishing touches like the odd rug or carpet vacuuming.

The couple were not home by four as expected and by seven the group were anxious so Chris phoned the airport to see if the plane had been delayed for some reason. The girl at the airport terminal desk was quite relieved that someone had rung. There was a problem and they could not contact any relatives.

"What did they say?" asked Matty while they were driving to the airport.

It seemed that there had been some sort of mishap and they thought that Robert, Mr Frimble to them, had boarded another plane. Chris continued, Karen was so distraught that a doctor was called and she was given some sedation and they took her to hospital. Miss Friedland will tell us more when we arrive. Miss Freidland, pleasant but factual, told them that Mr and Mrs Frimble had boarded the flight 306. Mrs Frimble had apparently had a bad flight over to the states and had taken some form of sleeping draught to help her on the way back. Shortly before landing the air stewardess had awoken Mrs Frimble to ask her to put a seat belt on and that is the first time that Mr Frimble was known to be missing. The stewards and stewardesses checked every locker and toilet and room on the plane but he was not to be found. There was however a pile of clothes similar to those Mr Frimble had been wearing in a neat pile at the back of the plane. Mrs Frimble became very distraught and the crew had to restrain her while the plane landed. Upon landing, no one including the crew were allowed to leave the plane and a police search team had no success. A doctor was called to Mrs Frimble who was understandably still distraught and had to be sectioned there and then. They took her to Fir Tree hospital. "We must go to her," said Matty.

"What about their luggage," said Chris.

"I am afraid that all their possessions are now in the hands of the police. A sergeant Hoskins can be the one to assist you there."

This seems incredible but it is just like one of those invisible man films and he has somehow divested himself of clothing and got off the plane without anyone seeing or hearing him.

The next day Matty and Chris went to the hospital, Karen was still in her catatonic state and only responding to food, when it was spoon fed like a baby. Matty was in floods of tears remembering the carefree Karen that had come into their lives. She had everything to live for and it appeared, someone to share the happiness with. All blasted to crumbs without warning.

Chris asked the doctor in charge what was best for her. His recommendation for her in her present condition was to be in familiar surroundings with people she knew and trusted and hope that with some mild medication she may 'come out of the state' that her mind had concluded she is best protected in.

They arranged for her to be transferred to home or rather to Chris and Matty's part of the house which had been familiar to her and the four of them would take turns to watch over her when there were no nursing staff available.

The ambulance was duly organised and they were amazed that it was escorted by a police car.

The ambulance men put her into Chris and Matty's room where they felt it was best for her, they had not anticipated that a policewoman would have to be in the room at all times. It was explained that for the time being they had a missing person, maybe a murder suspect, they had no way of knowing what was happening therefore had to take precautions. There was a shift of four policewomen and they would look after themselves if they could use the facilities.

The local doctor had been kept fully informed and was to visit daily, to administer the medication in the form of an injection at this time. He also arranged for a district nurse to call on a twice daily basis to carry out necessary cleaning etc.

After a week it was clear to the police force that she was indeed not trying to pull the wool over their eyes and the police watch was withdrawn. Karen seemed to be just a robotic person that ate and drank when prompted and as far as they could tell the foetus was not affected in any way.

Tirelessly, the four took their turn at waiting for her to 'snap' out of it. week after week and the doctor lowered the level of sedation to practically nil with no ill effects. The nurses were brilliant with her, so patient and caring.

The Police Inspector arrived one day to try and unravel some of the threads in this case that had them completely baffled.

Did anyone know why Robert Frimble had transferred £ 500,000 to an old account in his brother's name in the states. No one knew.

Did anyone know where that sort of money plus another £ 500,000 could have been obtained? Chris remembered that

Robert had talked about a land deal they had done but that was a year ago he thought.

Had anyone any idea of any solicitors that were involved in this land deal.

"Well," said Matty she was a solicitor herself, worked for, I can't remember their name but Sir Henry is Head of Chambers it is in Melfort."

"We will find him."

"Does anyone know of the existence of any wills for either Mr Robert Frimble or Mrs Karen Frimble?"

They looked at each other, not as far as we know but why should we.

"Quite."

"Oh lastly, for now, you have a son in Africa I believe?" "You are very well-informed Inspector, even we are not certain of his whereabouts. He is somewhere in the wilderness as a paediatric surgeon correcting birth malformations, helping children with cleft palates and other genetic defects.. He was due to come back to England a couple of years ago but decided to remain in post. He has a permanent post option in a London clinic whenever he wishes to return."

The Inspector called in at the solicitors to find another dead end. Apparently, Sir Henry had succumbed to a seizure and a brain bleed and would not last the night.

While at the office, he spoke to Matthew, but Matthew could only remember that Sir Henry had a Sir Peter with him in the office on two occasions and after the last occasion Karen left her post.

Matthew had no knowledge of the meeting.

"Where could I contact this Sir Peter?"

"Only through a medium I am afraid, he died six months ago, Sir Henry and I went to his funeral. Shot himself by all accounts, starting to clean a shotgun."

"Are there any records of a major land deal at or about that time."

"None recorded but Sir Peter was known to be 'a one-off ' and had full control of the Pressguard account as well as a personal 'fund' if you get my meaning.

Months after the plane incident as it was known there was one night when Chris, who had been working hard in the garden, fell asleep on his watch, when he awoke Karen was missing. He quickly called the other two and they searched only to find Karen sitting in the corner of the room on Megan's chair, with a bundle of rags on her knee. Matty noticed a movement and as Isobel went forward there was a cry. It was more than a something; it was a baby!!! As she leaned forward, she could see the bundle moving but she could also see that Karen was white and still.

Prising the baby from the rags she let out a stifled cry. The baby had a huge birthmark on her neck and shoulder. Issie knew now what had to be done and she remembered the words under the lych gate.

'In your hearts and your hands lies her destiny, help the new MEGAN.

Roger conducted the service at the church and the coffin was buried in the Frimble area. Matty and Issie had asked that the coffin lid be left off the previous night in the church. They were sure a reunion would have taken place.

It was those last words under the Lych gate. In your hearts and hands lies her destiny…help the new Megan.

Kevin came home that very next day to the delight of Matty and of course as a surgeon he took one look at Megan and told Issie and Matty that he could sort that out in his new surgery.

Twenty-five years on from that date, Megan qualified as a paediatric surgeon specialising on birthmark removal and defects. She became a world renowned surgeon in her own right. She also chose to marry a man twenty years her senior and they had three children, a girl and twin boys. The girl was called Karen and the boys were called James and Henry.

Megan and Kevin inherited a half-moon each and just as Derek had wanted, the circle of life was complete, life goes round.

THE MOON WOULD BE SHINING ON THE MOON HOUSE FOREVER.

—-/—
_/_